SILVER BULLET

Jack Dillon Dublin Tale 4

Second Edition

SILVER BULLET

Jack Dillon Dublin Tale 4
Second Edition

Mike Faricy

Library of Congress Control Number: 2023920346
paperback ISBN: 978-1-962080-67-5
e-Book ISBN: 978-1-962080-68-2

MJF Publishing books may be purchased for education, Business, or promotional use. For information on bulk purchases, please contact the author directly at mikefaricyauthor@gmail.com

Published by

MJF Publishing
https://www.mikefaricybooks.com

ACKNOWLEDGMENTS

I would like to thank the following people for their help & support: Special thanks to Nick, Roy, Julie, Mittie, and Toui for their hard work, cheerful patience and positive feedback. I would like to thank family and friends for their encouragement and unqualified support. Special thanks to Maggie, Jed, Schatz, Pat, Av, Emily and Pat, for not rolling their eyes, at least when I was there. Most of all, to my wife, Teresa, whose belief, support and inspiration has, from day one, never waned.

"You Americans, you're all fecking nuts."

~Enda Murray

ONE

Dillon carried the ice bucket up into Lin's bedroom and set it on the end table. He was barechested and wearing an unbuckled pair of jeans. It was barely one in the afternoon, but she had the curtains pulled, which cast the room into darkness. Now the only illumination came from the three scented candles flickering on her dresser. He unzipped his jeans and slowly slid them down his hips.

She gave him a few seconds of applause, giggled, and sat up, letting the linen sheet fall away, exposing her attributes. He quickly climbed into bed. She leaned over, gave him a long, lingering kiss, then nibbled his ear lobe for a moment before she straightened up. He reached across the pillow to the ice bucket on the end table and removed the bottle of wine. "Say when," he said, pouring the sparkling Portuguese white into the crystal flute she held.

Droplets of ice-cold condensation dripped onto her thigh, and her nipples immediately grew erect.

"Oh, whoa, whoa, that's enough." She gazed down at her chest, moved her shoulders from side to side, then giggled again and said, "Oh God, now look what you made me do, party hats."

"Looks like the perfect way to spend a Saturday afternoon," he said, then clicked glasses with her and toasted. "To your beauty, Lin. And you are really and truly beautiful."

"I bet you say that to all the naked girls you drink with in bed," she laughed, and they clinked glasses again.

"No, I mean it. Thanks for inviting me over. It's the first day off I've had since, well, forever. What could be better than spending it with you this afternoon and—"

"All afternoon," she said.

"It's just more than I ever could have hoped for."

"Are you kidding?" she said. "God, the promise of an entire afternoon of debauchery and then you cooking me dinner tonight. How could I refuse? This just might well be the beginning of some—"

He visibly cringed at the sudden sound of his cellphone.

"Don't answer that?" she said.

He grabbed his jeans off the floor, fumbling for a moment in search of his cellphone. The irritating sound immediately pushed the passion out of the room. He pulled his cellphone out of the pocket and glanced at the screen. McCabe, damn it, and it was supposed to be his day off.

"Oh please, don't answer, Jack. It can't be good news." She wedged the crystal glass between her breasts, hands-free, and held her arms out.

"Yeah," he answered.

"Dillon, catch you at a bad time?"

He looked over at Lin. She pulled the glass out from between her breasts, took a sip of wine, smiled, slowly shook her breasts from side to side, and raised her eyebrows suggestively.

"Dillon, are you there?"

He turned around, sat on the edge of the bed, and attempted to concentrate on McCabe's voice. He tried to ignore Lin's hand rubbing his shoulder but seemed to be failing. She began to purr like a kitten, then suddenly she was nibbling along his neck, half-whispering indecent suggestions into his ear as she rubbed her body against his back. She slowly began to move her free hand down his chest, lingering on his stomach for just the briefest of moments.

"Turn down that damn television, for God's sake. What the hell are you watching anyway? Listen, there's been an incident. Initial report is it's an American, not much else to go on at the moment. We're still in a state of flux. You know where The Stag's Head is?"

Dillon rose from the bed, stepped out of the bedroom, and stood in the hall. He gave a quick glance back into the bedroom.

Lin flashed a set of eyes that seemed to glow in the dark and had suddenly lost any pretense of romance.

"Hello? Dillon, are you there? Are you listening? I said, do you know where the Stag's Head is?"

"Yes, I know where the Stag's Head is, just off Dame Street. However, need I remind you, I'm off today. In fact, I'm supposed to be off for the next three days. As a matter of fact, this is my first day off in over two and a half weeks and you promised I could have seventy-two hours to rest up. I think the term you used was *Rejuvenate my inner soul* or some such nonsense, and I was just about to commence with that exact undertaking."

"Yes, well forget about that for the time being, and you're right, for a change, it was nonsense. What? Oh, Dillon, hang on for a second, I'm about to get an update here. Just a minute."

Dillon could hear a conversation, but couldn't make out what was being said. He was in the process of coming up with a reason, maybe come up with a number of reasons why he couldn't possibly join McCabe. He didn't feel the need to mention he had an afternoon and evening scheduled with nympho nurse Lin when McCabe suddenly came back on the line.

"All right, sorry about that, Dillon. This has just been upgraded to top priority. We'll need you here just as fast as possible. Does the name Kevin Fitzwilliam mean anything to you?"

"No, can't say that it rings a bell. To tell you the truth, sir, I'm not sure I'd be at my best. Does the term exhausted—"

"What about Brian Fitzwilliam?"

"Never heard of either one. Look—"

"Brian is apparently Kevin's father. I hasten to add he's also a Senator from your state of Missouri. One would think you'd care at least enough to know who your Senator is—"

"I'm from Minnesota, originally, haven't lived there for over ten years and I certainly—"

"We're in the process of getting the area sealed off. I'll expect you here in the next twenty minutes," McCabe said. "Look for me, I won't have time to seek the likes of you out."

"Twenty minutes—" Dillon started to protest, but McCabe had already hung up the phone.

Dillon gave a longing look at Lin. Just now, she was standing at the end of the bed with her hands on her hips. He pictured her gorgeous figure in a variety of positions. It was supposed to be the perfect afternoon, and actually, it was, at least up until McCabe had inserted himself. He seemed suddenly resigned to the fact that he would have to take a raincheck on the afternoon's festivities. He stepped back into the bedroom, holding his cellphone behind his back.

"No, don't tell me."

"Maybe if we hurry, we could at least—"

"So, you're going back to work? You're apparently not interested," she said striking a pose.

"I'm afraid I have to, it's some American, down by the Stag's Head, I guess, I don't know what happened exactly, but they want me there. And, I am interested, very interested. Maybe we could just grab a quickie and—"

"Oh, not to worry, don't let me hold you up," she said and strutted around to the far side of the bed. She bent down, striking a pose for a long moment before throwing his jeans and shirt across the bed to him. She tossed his socks and boxers next, this time a bit more forcefully, then turned around and pulled open a dresser drawer.

"Look, Lin, no one is more disappointed than me. Honest. I'm really sorry. Maybe, I can do whatever it is I have to do, and then I could hurry back here, and we can pick up where we left off. Why don't you just have another little glass of wine and I could—"

"Oh please, don't bother on my account. Besides, I've got other plans," she said and rummaged around for a second or two in the open drawer. She pulled out a large red vibrator, spun around to face him, and turned it on. The thing made an audible sound. She glared at Dillon, then slowly turned the dial at the base so that it actually grew louder until he could see the thing vibrating back and forth in her hand. She raised her eyebrows and glared.

"Lin, I'll be back just as soon as I can."

"Shame you can't stay for the party, but you better get going. I wouldn't want you to be late."

"Look, Lin, I'm really sorry."

"Get going, you wanker. I've got other plans," she said, then crawled across the bed, pulled the three pillows one on top of the other, and leaned back. She grabbed her crystal glass, drained it in one long swallow and said, "Go on, I feel the need for some privacy."

He left a brief note consisting of an apology and a bit of groveling on her dining room table. He wrote the note on the back of an envelope using a red color crayon since that was the only thing he could find. He hinted at an international emergency, hoping that would calm her explosive temper, then quietly closed the door behind him and hurried to his car. Unfortunately, his car, a 2007 Opel Corsa, started on the third try, and he drove off toward the city center and Dame Street, thinking about Lin and what she might be doing at that exact moment. He fantasized all the way into the city center, which did nothing to alleviate his growing sense of frustration.

TWO

The Stag's Head pub was near the Temple Bar district, one of a number of classic pubs in Dublin, a city filled with classic pubs. The place had been pouring pints since 1770, and Dillon had been there a number of times, although he'd never think of referring to himself as a regular.

Dublin city was notorious for its lack of parking, and he pulled onto a side street a few blocks away from the Stag's Head. He spent the better part of ten minutes inching back and forth between two parked cars until he was satisfied he more or less had the parking space and wouldn't get a ticket or be clamped. Then, just to be sure, he placed his An Garda Síochána sign, complete with elaborate Garda logo, on the dashboard. The name in Irish translated to "The Guardian of the Peace," the Irish cops. A woman carrying a shopping bag walked past, glanced at the sign on the dash, looked at the whiskey shop he'd parked in front of, and wrinkled her nose in disgust.

"Taking another spot from the taxpayer, I see."

"I'm working a case."

"Sure you are, a case of Jameson, no doubt," she said and continued on.

He wove his way through the tangle of streets, until he got semi-lost, realized he was off by one street, then backtracked until he came to Dame Lane. He could see the Stag's Head pub, just up ahead at the corner of Dame Lane and Dame Court. White tape with blue letters extended across Dame Lane halting all pedestrian traffic. As he drew closer, he could read the tape: "DO NOT CROSS" in English and Irish. A small crowd milled around on one side of the tape while two uniformed Garda stood on the other side, smiling and shaking their heads 'no' to just about every question they were asked.

Dillon stepped through the crowd of about a dozen onlookers and waved one of the Guards over. They wore blue uniforms and bright florescent green vests. The back of the vest was blue with the word 'GARDA' in white letters. The man approaching Dillon had red hair and a ready smile.

"Yes sir, how may I help?" he said.

Dillon held out his ID and said, "US Marshal Jack Dillon. I got a call from DCI McCabe about a half-hour ago, interrupting what was turning out to be a perfect afternoon with a gorgeous woman who just couldn't get enough of me."

The Guard grinned, glanced at Dillon's ID, and said, "Sounds like the work of McCabe. Come on in. You'll find him down there somewhere. He's wearing a blue windbreaker with a Dublin logo on the left breast if memory serves."

"Thanks," Dillon said, ducked under the tape and headed down the lane.

Halfway down the lane, a man who looked familiar nodded and said, "Dillon," then went back to talking to the woman next to him.

There was a side entrance to the Stag's Head with a sign above the door that read "Lounge." Some fool had spray-painted illegible graffiti on the red brick next to the entrance. On the opposite side of the entrance, sixty or seventy beer barrels were double-stacked. Presumably they were empty and waiting for pick-up. The barrels ran almost the length of the building.

At the far end of the stack of barrels, a couple of white nylon screens had been set up to block vision and isolate the area. Two individuals in white hazmat suits were kneeling next to the screens, presumably over the body. A third was taking photographs. A pair of legs extended just beyond the screen, actually, just a hint of black jeans with both feet visible. The feet appeared to be wearing what looked like black shoes with a white Nike swoosh, the Nike logo, along the side. A small crowd was gathered further down, milling back and forth on the far side of more blue and white tape telling people not to cross. Maybe half the people were sipping from pint glasses as they watched.

He spotted McCabe about twenty feet away from the body, with his back toward Dillon. He was talking to two other individuals, both of whom looked familiar, and one of whom Dillon remembered, Paddy Suel. He hurried over to the three of them. Suel gave him a nod as he approached, causing McCabe to turn around.

"Well, well, if it isn't Marshal Dillon, and almost on time, imagine my surprise," McCabe said.

"Thanks for including me," Dillon said, not meaning a word of it, then shook Suel's extended hand. "Good to see you again, Paddy."

"Likewise. I think you've met Derm Crowley before," Suel said, saving Dillon the trouble of asking a name.

"Yeah, we've met before. Nice to see you again, Derm."

"Dillon," Crowley said as they shook hands.

"Chief Inspector," Dillon said and extended his hand to McCabe. "Always a pleasure."

"Appreciate you coming, Dillon. Sorry to interrupt your time off almost before it started, but this is going to be a priority. We've—" McCabe suddenly wrinkled his nose a couple of times, leaned slightly closer to Dillon, and sniffed. "New perfume, Dillon? Not sure it suits you, although it's very nice."

Suel and Crowley chuckled.

"Well, I was in the midst of trying to relax."

"This will be much more fun," Suel said.

"Mmm-mmm," McCabe said, sounding unimpressed. "Here's what we have thus far." McCabe held up a pocket-sized notebook and began to read. "An

American male, shot once in the right side. Passport in possession identifies him as one Kevin Fitzwilliam, age twenty-three. A business card attached to his passport lists US Senator Brian Fitzwilliam from the state of Missouri. A quick check verifies the deceased as a son."

"Has the US embassy been informed yet?"

"Not yet," McCabe said. "But we're going to have to do so very shortly. As part of their procedure, they'll be sending someone over who will no doubt want to participate in the investigation. Be nice to have as much information as possible prior to that."

"Any idea who they'll send?"

McCabe shook his head, then sort of glanced around. "Damned strange, middle of the day. A pleasant day at that."

"Eyewitnesses?" Dillon asked.

"No, at least none that have come forward. A half-dozen folks who claim to have heard the shot, but thus far no one who actually saw the incident. We've got a team interviewing now and taking down information. No description of the shooter, although the shot appears to have been at close range. I'm going to gamble and guess a small-caliber weapon. God bless them for wanting to help, but I fear those who said they heard the shot may be imagining."

"I'm going to need you to contact the embassy before I go through channels and ask for anything on the victim," Dillon said. "Once I go through channels, I can then personally contact someone to see if there's any additional information on the individual. Fitzwilliam, you said?"

"Yes," McCabe said, "Kevin Fitzwilliam."

"I wonder if he was a student. Maybe at Trinity or DCU."

"Or just a tourist here for a week or two," Crowley added.

"If I might suggest, sir," Suel said. "Let's get in touch with the university and colleges in Dublin, then elsewhere, see if the lad's name comes up anywhere. Also hotels, and the airlines, right now, any information would be helpful."

"The embassy may have all of that, certainly if he was a student. With the father serving in the US Senate, they may have a little tighter hold on this than a normal student or tourist."

"Normal," Crowley laughed.

"Right," McCabe said and pulled out his cellphone. "I'll instruct the office to contact the embassy. They'll have my number and get back to me. With the political link, this is going to take on a life of its own in very short order. Crowley, get moving on colleges and universities. Suel, you and Dillon examine the site, but for God's sake, stay out of the way. I'll want you touching base with the morgue, find out when that autopsy will be scheduled. We'll need a preliminary report just as soon as possible. I want answers, people. This is going to be kicked upstairs very quickly. I don't intend to be left grabbing my ankles."

THREE

McCabe was standing off to the side on the phone, his fourth or fifth call in the past ten minutes. Dillon had given up counting. He seemed to be looking just a little more stressed with every call, so much for not grabbing his ankles.

Dillon and Paddy Suel had been standing back, maybe fifteen feet, taking note of the surrounding area. The crowds at the taped-off area at either end of the lane continued to grow, and four more Garda had arrived to keep people back.

Although the Lounge door to the Stag's Head had been closed, the main pub was still serving. Just across the courtyard, the Dame Tavern was open for business as well. It was approaching two o'clock, and from now until closing time, both places would be full. Add to that a gorgeous sunny day following three days of drizzle, and you knew why the crowds at either end of the taped-off area were now six deep, a number of them sipping pints. The level of laughter and comments had picked up, and once or twice, someone cursed. At this rate, in another hour or so, things could start to get serious. It would only take one or two jerks to set the mood off in the wrong direction.

"McCabe said the kid was twenty-three?" Suel asked.

"Yeah," Dillon replied.

"Bit of a babyface. I would have pegged him for about fifteen except for that wisp of a beard."

Two uniformed Guards were cautiously searching alongside the line of empty beer barrels. The people in hazmat suits kneeling and examining the body looked to be finishing up. One of them stepped back and pulled the mask away, revealing a woman's face. She said something to her partner, then headed toward Dillon and Suel. The photographer continued taking pictures from various angles.

"How's it going, Doc?" Suel said as she approached.

"Not the best of days when it starts out with something like this, Paddy." She pulled her hood back and shook her head, freeing up some neatly trimmed blonde hair, then unzipped the front of her hazmat suit.

"Woo-hoo-hoo, take it off, baby," an American accent called from somewhere in the crowd up near the front door to the Stag's Head. The comment brought a couple of chuckles, but far more heads turned and gave a disgusted look.

"You want me to go cuff that asshole and hang him from the lamp post?" Dillon asked.

"No, best not, damage to public property, it'll just result in a fine," Suel said. "Jack, this is one of our medical examiners, Doctor Katie Costello. This is US Marshal Jack Dillon. He's been assigned—"

"Please to meet you, Marshal. I've heard all sorts of stories," she said and smiled.

"None of them true, I'm actually a very nice guy."

"Is he, Paddy?"

"That remains to be seen."

"Please, call me Jack," Dillon said.

"Only if you call me Katie."

"So?" Suel asked.

"Let me show you," Katie said.

They followed her over to the body just as the guy taking pictures stepped back, and pulled his mask off. "All finished, Jerry?" she asked.

"Yeah, I've got it. All yours. Feel free to move him."

She stepped alongside the body and crouched down. The face appeared even younger close up. Just the slightest thin wisp of a beard, maybe the size of a fifty-cent piece, covered the area just beneath the chin.

The black jeans had two supposed tears on the upper thigh of the left leg. They weren't real tears, but rather manufactured distress. White bleached-out spots ran up and down the legs to make the jeans appear worn. It was possible it was all homemade, the bleach spots and the tears, but Dillon suspected they were expensive designer jeans and made a mental note to check on it. The silkscreened t-shirt displayed worn-looking letters that read, "U2 UNDER THE BLOOD RED SKY. 1983". The letters were silkscreened to appear old-looking and were white with the exception of the word "BLOOD," which was printed in a worn looking red. Again, the t-shirt, like the jeans, was manufactured to appear worn. The left side of the victim's face looked like he might have been punched. Dillon wondered if perhaps there had been some sort of fight. Could he have been the victim of a mugging gone bad?

Katie slipped a hand beneath the victim's shoulder and the middle of his back and gently rolled him partially over onto his left side. There, just below the right armpit and alongside the victim's arm, was a very modest amount of blood. Katie carefully edged the t-shirt up.

"You look closely, you can see some stippling around the wound, the weapon was close, very close, when fired. It wouldn't have been right up against the body, but no more than six inches away, probably a lot closer than that. There's no exit wound, so the pathologist should be able to recover the round."

"What about the bruising along the side of the face?" Suel asked.

"Consistent with bouncing his head off the brick wall. My assessment, someone is up close, very close, fires, he jerks or half jumps against the brick wall, and then he collapses onto the stone pavement. If I had to hazard a guess, I'd say he was dead before he hit the ground. My educated guess to cause of death, is a small-caliber round to the heart, death would have occurred almost immediately. The autopsy should confirm that.”

“Chief Inspector,” one of the Guards searching along the length of empty beer barrels called. He was down on one knee and held what looked like an evidence bag in his hand.

“Let me call you back,” McCabe said into his phone as he hurried past. Dillon, Suel, and Costello quickly followed.

“I’d say this is it, sir,” the Guard said, looking down at a shiny cartridge resting against the base of a beer barrel.

“Okay, let’s all step back. Jerry,” McCabe called over to the photographer. “If we could get photos of this from every angle.”

Jerry was already on his way over and started taking pictures without saying a word. He took at least a half-dozen shots, then stepped over to McCabe and said, “We’re all finished with the initial examination, sir. Might be the best idea to have the body removed.” He glanced down the lane toward the crowd near the door to the Stag’s Head, now about twelve people deep. Some guy was just delivering a fresh round of pint glasses to four of his pals, the murder scene apparently serving as the afternoon’s entertainment.

“They’re just waiting around the corner for the word,” McCabe said, then pulled his phone out and stepped to the side.

"You want to bag this or is it all right if I do?" the Guard who'd discovered the round said.

"Let me get it," Katie Costello said and pulled a plastic bag from her hazmat suit. She shook the bag a couple of times to open it. She pulled a small metal device from a breast pocket. The device looked almost like a pen, although it was one solid piece. She knelt down and inserted the device in the open end of the cartridge, raised it and examined it closely for a long moment before she dropped it in the bag, then zip-locked the bag closed. She rose to her feet and examined the cartridge as Suel, Dillon and the Guard closed in around her.

"What do you make of this?" she asked. The cartridge was silver-colored rather than brass.

"Small caliber," Suel said.

Dillon waited a moment, then said, "May I?" Costello handed him the bag, and he looked at it closely, turning it over a couple of times and examining the cartridge from all angles.

"Educated guess is the caliber is a 380 ACP. This looks to be a Winchester Silver Tip."

"ACP?" the Guard looked up and asked.

"Automatic Colt Pistol. See how there's no rim on the back of the cartridge? It's straight-walled. These first became popular back in the early 90s. It's a round for a very small pistol that could easily fit in your hand or a purse. You can carry them tucked into a belt, and no one would be the wiser. The pistol's maybe just an inch and a half wide, five, five and a half inches long. The rules vary from state to state, but you can get a conceal and carry permit anywhere in the US. Small pistols, like the one this cartridge came from, just flew off the shelves. I know things are a lot stricter here. Don't you have to register with the local Guardai station to even own a weapon?"

"Yes, you do," Suel said. "I'd say looking for the purchase of a small-caliber piece like this the list will be fairly short. We may have just gotten our first break. Let me get someone checking on that. You'll log that in, Katie?"

She nodded.

FOUR

A fluorescent green ambulance arrived at the far end of the lane, maybe ten minutes later. Its lights were flashing, and it sounded the siren a couple of times to get the crowd to step aside. One guy was either deaf or a complete jerk and didn't move until a Guard politely took his arm and pulled him to the side. The ambulance drove down the lane past Dillon and the others, past the line of empty beer barrels, and stopped just beyond the white nylon screens.

Two guys in dark blue trousers and shirts jumped out from either side of the ambulance, hurried to the back, and opened the set of double doors. Dublin firefighters. One of them stepped inside, and a moment later, they had a gurney on the ground and were wheeling it over to where Kevin Fitzwilliam's body lay. McCabe, on the phone again with someone, hurried past Dillon and Suel, waving at the ambulance crew as he approached. The crowds on either end of the lane grew quiet.

Dillon and Suel waited for a moment, then followed up behind. As they approached, McCabe was in the process of issuing instructions. Based on the faces of the ambulance crew, they'd heard the words a thousand times before.

"The city morgue, it's been moved up onto Drumcondra Road and Griffith Ave," McCabe was saying.

"Yes, sir, three or four years ago, wasn't it Tommy?" the driver asked his partner.

"Four years for sure, maybe more. We've been there a few thousand times. I think we can find our way."

"Christ. McCabe is up to ninety," Suel said under his breath.

They deftly placed the body into a black bodybag, zipped it shut, then grabbing onto the handles at either end, hoisted it up onto the gurney.

"You'll be going up to the morgue?" the driver asked McCabe. As he spoke, they each wrapped a strap over the bodybag in a practiced fashion, then cinched it tight to secure it to the gurney.

"No, DI Suel and Marshal Dillon will be headed up there," McCabe said and gave a nod in Suel's direction.

"We should be up there in fifteen minutes. We've another pick-up, on the north side in Finglas. That one's hanging by a rope...."

"No, I think they said a bedsheet," his partner replied.

"Anyway, we'll drop the lad off first. I know you want them on it just as soon as possible. Enjoy the rest of your day, gentlemen," the driver said, then gave a nod and they wheeled the gurney over to the open rear doors on the ambulance and loaded the gurney into the back in one fluid motion. They closed the rear doors and headed up to the cab. The rear of the ambulance was the same florescent green color as the rest of the vehicle, only with broad orange stripes running across either door at a forty-five-degree angle and meeting in the middle to form a right angle. The word "AMBULANCE," in case anyone had a doubt, was written in capital letters across the top of the double doors.

The flashing lights were suddenly turned back on. The siren sounded a couple of blurps, and the crowd out in front of the Stag's Head immediately parted, making a wide opening so they could drive through. A few people in the crowd made the sign of the cross as it slowly passed.

"Suel," McCabe said. "You and Dillon head up to the morgue. Let me know when you've got something. I'm headed back to the office to meet with the team from the US Embassy."

"I'm parked a couple of blocks away," Dillon said to Suel. "I'll meet you over there."

It took him a good fifteen minutes to find his car. At least half that time was spent searching up and down the wrong street. When he did find it, some not-so-gifted artist had spray-painted the word "Wanker" in black on the driver's door just below the official An Garda Síochána sign he'd placed on the dashboard.

FIVE

Dillon circled back past Stephen's Green, went down a couple of blocks and took a left, crossed the Liffey, and turned onto Drumcondra a short bit later. Traffic was bumper to bumper, and it took him a good twenty minutes before he made it up to Griffith Avenue. He pulled up onto the boulevard, leaving a muddy tire track in the process, then climbed out and locked the car door. He ran a finger across the spray-painted graffiti on the driver's door in the odd hope it might somehow rub off. It didn't. He waited for a car to pass, then hurried across the street to the two-story brick building with the black wrought iron fence—Dublin city morgue.

Suel was standing in the reception area paging through a leaflet advertising Glasnevin cemetery. He looked up as Dillon came through the front door.

"The only bit of land I own. Three cemetery plots out in Sligo near the home place. I'd guess they're a lot dearer in Glasnevin," Suel said and tossed the leaflet back in the rack bolted to the wall

A phone rang just behind the glass partition at the receptionist desk. The woman at the desk picked up on the second ring. Dillon could hear the sound of her voice, but couldn't make out what she was saying. Whatever it was, the conversation was very short. She stood, then leaned forward toward the louvered metal disk embedded in the center of the window.

"Detective Suel, Doctor Byrne is ready for you in her office. You know the way?"

"I do, Madeline, not to worry, we'll walk back," he said, then headed for a door opposite the receptionist counter. As he approached, Madeline pushed a button, and an audible buzz sounded. Suel pulled the door open and held it for Dillon, who stepped inside. The hall was painted a soft white color and had a series of framed watercolors depicting various Dublin scenes hanging at regular intervals along the length of the hallway. Various doors along the hall opened into a number of moderate-sized offices. Alicia Byrne's office was halfway down the hall. The nameplate on the door read,

Dr. Alicia Byrne

Pathologist

The door was closed, and Suel knocked then opened the door just as a female voice called out, "Come in."

She was an attractive brunette whom Dillon had met a couple of times before, always under case-related circumstances. Just now, she was sitting at her desk, wearing a white lab coat and shaking a tea bag over her steaming mug. She dropped the tea bag into a wastebasket along the side of her desk. She picked up a round, choc-olate-covered biscuit, dipped it into her tea mug, and placed the entire thing in her mouth.

"Ummm, come on in, gentlemen, and grab a seat. I'm famished, and this emergency you've deposited on our doorstep is going to have me here until late tonight. You want a biscuit or a tea?"

Suel shook his head.

"No thanks," Dillon said.

"Good to see you again," she said, dipping another biscuit into her tea. "So, what do we have?"

"Shooting victim, American. Turns out he's the son of a U.S. Senator," Suel said.

"Oh, so that's the rush, is it?" she said, then put the biscuit into her mouth, chewed, swallowed, and grabbed another biscuit.

"Seems to be a small-caliber round. The M.E. sug-gested it entered the heart, said death may have been in-stantaneous."

"Who was the M.E.?" she asked through a mouth filled with biscuit.

"Costello."

She nodded, swallowed, and said, "She's good. All right, I'll be in there in the next twenty minutes. I can text you when I'm close to being finished, give you a preliminary. I'll get the paperwork going tonight. I better get moving, we might still be able to get tissue samples in for testing with today's date, which will get them back just that much faster," she said. She stood as she spoke and brushed imaginary crumbs from off the front of her lab coat.

"We'll wait to hear from you. Thanks in advance for working late," Suel said.

"And thank you in advance for the nice bottle of wine you're going to bring me, a red." She smiled. "The both of you."

"Our pleasure," Dillon said and followed Suel out of the office. They headed back down the hallway toward the front. Doctor Byrne went in the opposite direction, pulling off her lab coat as she headed down the hall.

SIX

Dillon stood on the sidewalk alongside Suel's car. Suel had just unlocked the door, but the moment the locks chirped, he turned to face Dillon. "Jack, what do you think the odds are this was a random shooting?"

"Not as great as it would be if this had happened back in the States," Dillon said.

"We'll need to look at CCTV images see if we can spot him. I don't know maybe there was someone with him."

"God, it couldn't be that easy, could it?" Dillon said, sounding hopeful.

"Once we get a handle on what he was doing over here, that should open the possibility of maybe an acquaintance, a classmate, roommate, someone he met on the plane coming over. Who the hell knows?"

Dillon shook his head and exhaled in response.

"Drugs?" Suel asked.

"You know, anything's possible at this stage. But, my first reaction, he was nicely dressed. He…."

"Jeans and a t-shirt?"

"Those were designer jeans. Both the jeans and the U2 t-shirt were designed to look old and worn. This generation, they pay extra for that, pay big dollars. Those jeans, they could easily run a couple hundred bucks."

"God, I'm so out of it nowadays," Suel said. "Hey, I'll see you back at the office. With any luck we'll have some tapes to start looking at."

"I'm going to swing by my place, let Lucifer out for a minute or two. I've a feeling it may be a late night." He crossed the street to his car, noticed the muddy tire tread he'd left on someone's boulevard, and thought for half a moment that the "Wanker" spray-painted on the door of his car might not be too far from the truth.

He lived no more than five or ten minutes from the morgue. He drove down Griffith Avenue, up Ballymun Road, then turned on St. Pappins Road to Dean Swift. He pulled in front and parked halfway over the sidewalk so cars could get past and still leave room for someone on the footpath.

When he opened the door, Lucifer, his black dog, stood just inside the front entry. The day's mail had been dropped through the slot in the door, and it appeared that Lucifer had relieved himself on the envelopes.

"Damn it, Lucifer. I told you I'd be back to let you out."

The dog seemed to wrinkle its nose, then hopped out the door and onto the lawn. He circled once or twice, then squatted and stared at Dillon while he left a major deposit on the lawn. Dillon left the door open, then picked up the four stained and dripping envelopes off the floor, holding them at the very corner between thumb and forefinger as he hurried into the kitchen.

He tossed the envelopes into the kitchen sink and pulled the wastebasket over. Fortunately, three of the four envelopes were solicitations from a cable provider, the local church, and an insurance company. The fourth envelope was an invitation to a dinner party at Billy and Anne Morley's home. Unfortunately, the party, just a few doors down, had happened last night. He left the invitation in the sink, pulled out his phone, and dialed the RSVP number.

"Hi, Jack," Anne answered after a few rings. "We missed you last night. Working on some top-secret case?"

"Actually no, I just got the invitation in today's mail. Sorry. I would have enjoyed seeing everyone. I'm hoping you'll give me a rain check."

"Always. You busy tonight? It's just leftovers, but we'd love to see you."

"Thanks, Anne, but unfortunately, they pulled me in on my day off to work a case. It's some—"

"Not that awful thing next to the Stag's Head?"

"How'd you know about that?"

"Just heard it on the news. Not much to tell other than it was a shooting. Want to give me an update?" she said, sounding hopeful.

"Wish I could, Anne, but that's about all I know at this point. I hear anything, you'll be the first I call."

She laughed at that, then said, "Yeah, sure, not to worry. I won't hold my breath. Listen, you stop over when you can, we'd love to see you. You could take Billy off my hands, give me a break from cleaning up the mess he leaves wherever he goes."

"Hopefully, one of these next days," he said and hung up. He debated calling Lin, but about all he could tell her after more apologies, was that he was still working. Better to give her another few days to just cool down.

He stuck his head out the door and whistled for Lucifer. The dog stuck his head out from between two bushes against the garden wall, waited a minute then hurried inside. Dillon filled the food and water dish, then opened a kitchen cabinet and pulled out a Milk-Bone dog treat.

Lucifer immediately sat at attention, slowly moving his head from side to side as Dillon held the Milk-Bone and moved it back and forth. After a few times back and forth, he tossed it up into the air, and Lucifer snatched it before it had a chance to hit the floor. He crunched and finished the treat in just a few bites, then sniffed around the floor for any wayward crumbs.

"Try and behave while I'm gone," Dillon said, then headed out the door.

SEVEN

It was a fairly fast drive to his office, maybe thirty minutes before the start of the rush hour traffic, and he'd made it through most of the lights. He pulled alongside the building then headed into the parking lot in the rear. He found a parking space in the middle of the lot, then climbed out, locked the car, and headed toward the rear door.

He grabbed his ID card and held it in front of the access control panel, then punched in his four-digit code when prompted. The lock snapped a moment later, and he pulled the door open. He draped the cord on his ID card around his neck and headed down the hallway. Up on the third floor, he went through the same process all over again before he entered the special branch office.

The room had originally been designed for probably half the amount of desks that were now crammed in it. Dillon, being the most recent member of the team, had been assigned the desk that, up until his arrival, had been the collection point for empty teacups, candy wrappers, and the occasional half-finished meal. Not much had changed.

He tossed a candy bar wrapper in the trash, and grabbed the three empty tea mugs off the edge of his desk, carried them into the break room and set them in the sink that was now so full of empty tea mugs that he had to stack the mugs on top of the plates and four mugs already in there.

He stepped out of the break room and hurried over to Paddy Suel's desk.

"Perfect timing," Suel said as Dillon approached. He clicked a half-dozen keys on his keyboard, which froze a grainy black and white image on his computer screen. He picked up a sheet of paper from his desk and handed it to Dillon. The sheet had two long lists of numbers.

"Burn a copy of that list, start at the bottom, and work your way up. I'm on the first tape at the top of the list, starting at 12:30. I've only been at it twenty minutes, but so far a big fat nothing. Security codes are the second column. These are from a variety of locations starting two blocks away. I figure we review sixty minutes on each tape. There's twenty-three tapes, which means we might be stuck here for a long time. I'm viewing at one and a half times normal speed. We don't find anything, we'll have to back up and view a four-block radius. Questions?"

"You got any popcorn?" Dillon joked.

"If only. Best get to it."

Dillon burned a copy of the list on the copy machine that was close to a thousand years old. Along the edge of the glass, someone had written in indelible marker at the halfway point, "Place Bum Here," apparently in an effort to encourage.

He gave the list back to Suel, returned to his desk, accessed the CCTV site, and logged on. He started with the tape at the bottom of the list and began viewing grainy black and white images that had been taken every five seconds as opposed to a constant video. They basically caught the activity on the sidewalk or lane. At best, the visual image was just barely okay. A digital readout giving date, time, and a numerical location on the tape appeared in the lower right-hand corner of each image. It took Dillon a few minutes to get used to a new image every five seconds before he sped up to one and a half times normal speed.

He checked each tape off as he worked his way up the list. It had been maybe two hours of focusing on grainy images, and Dillon was developing one hell of a headache when Suel yelled across the office, "Got him, Jack. Check this out."

Dillon stopped the tape he was watching, closed his eyes for a moment, and moved his head from side to side, causing his neck to crack before he rose out of his chair and hurried over to Suel's desk.

"Take a look. Thank God for that t-shirt he's wearing."

Dillon stared at the image frozen on Suel's screen. No question, it was Kevin Fitzwilliam. Unfortunately, he was alone. Suel clicked a key, and the next image appeared, Fitzwilliam, only closer and, unfortunately, still alone. Suel clicked on the next image, and the lane was empty except for a couple in the distance.

The couple looked to be in their early to mid-fifties. He was bald and had a gut protruding a substantial distance over his belt. She had dark hair and appeared to be in a lot better physical shape. They had their arms around one another's shoulder. Her free arm was extended out in front of the two of them, taking a cellphone photo. A selfie. His free arm appeared to hold a striped shopping bag, although it was impossible to determine from where at first glance.

"Christ, where in the hell is that?" Suel said. "I know the place, on the corner of Trinity Street just up from Keogh's. Come on, Dillon, help me out here. What's the name of the place?"

"How in the hell would I—"

"The Bankers, yeah, the Bankers Lounge," Suel half-shouted.

"Oh yeah, it's that red place right on the corner, right?"

"Yeah. I'll bet that fat plonker works in a bank, that's why they probably stopped to take the selfie. Within spitting distance from Trinity College. I wonder if your lad is a student?"

Suel ran back through a half dozen images, then forward again as the couple approached. About the time they stopped and paused, Fitzwilliam came into view. It appeared he passed them without giving a second look. A few images later, they began to return the way they'd come just as Fitzwilliam disappeared from view.

Suel clicked some more keys on the keyboard, and the printer beneath his desk sprung to life. "I'll print these off, then move ahead to the next camera."

Once he was into the new tape, he fast-forwarded for a couple of minutes, then stopped. "Oh Christ, too damn far," he growled and began to back up. He stopped just as Fitzwilliam came into view. He was on the screen for five different images. The fifth and final image was little more than his head from just the forehead up, but it was undoubtedly him. Unfortunately, he was once again alone, and there was no one else in any of the images.

"These are just outside the Academy of Photography," Suel said, sending the images to his printer. The printer started up a moment later, printing off all five images.

"Never been there," Dillon commented.

"Far too classy for the likes of you, no pornography. Let's move on to the next tape," Suel said and clicked a series of keys accessing the next tape. He brought the tape up, then sped through a number of images for a minute or two. "Shit, this is actually the courtyard. That doesn't work. We need the damn lane. Christ, don't they have a camera for that final stretch of the lane?" He clicked more keys, backed up slowly, went through the images one at a time. "Shit, shit, shit."

He clicked more keys, brought another tape up, and slowly began going through the images. No one looked familiar.

"Oh Christ, leave it to…Bollocks. Probably needed to save a hundred quid on some ridiculous budget. Damn it. Damn it. Damn it."

"Anything from the schools?" Dillon asked.

"Crowley?" Suel called. "Derm, you checking on the colleges?"

"Just about to," Crowley called back across the room. Everyone kept working at whatever task they were involved in as if people screaming back and forth was just an everyday occurrence, which, now that Dillon thought about it was probably the case.

"Check Trinity first. We got your man on CCTV heading toward the Stag's Head, alone. Maybe he was going to meet someone. Anyway, Trinity's the closest school. Start there."

EIGHT

Twenty minutes later, McCabe called Suel, Crowley, and Dillon into his office. When they entered, there was another man sitting in a chair opposite McCabe's desk. He didn't appear much older than mid-thirties with close-cropped blonde hair that was gelled and combed up in the front. He wore a dark blue suit, a starched white shirt, and a tie with a subdued pattern. He had a black wedding band on his left hand, tungsten steel most likely, and just behind the wedding band was a gold class ring with an onyx stone. If Dillon had to guess, he'd say he was a cop, probably from the Embassy.

"Gentlemen," McCabe said. "I'd like to introduce Special Agent Eric Bergman, with the US Embassy. He'll be assisting us in the Fitzwilliam investigation." McCabe sounded more like he was giving a directive, rather than just introducing Bergman.

Bergman stood as they entered, smiled, and nodded, then shook hands with Suel and Crowley as they introduced themselves. As they shook hands he gave a forceful shake to each man, and said, "Jack Bergman."

"Hi. Jack Dillon," Dillon said.

"Oh yeah, the Marshal," Bergman said, applying a tight squeeze to Dillon's hand. "Heard about you. Jack Bergman, Diplomatic Security Service."

"Why doesn't everybody grab a seat and we'll get started. Bergman, if I could have you start off, give us a general overview on the victim," McCabe said and handed a couple of pages that were stapled together across the desk to Bergman. "If you would be so kind as to bring everyone up-to-date on the information you've provided."

Bergman took the papers, quickly cleared his throat, and started in. "The oldest of four children, Kevin Brian Fitzwilliam was born 14 September 1994 in Jefferson City, Missouri." He looked up and said, "That's the Missouri state capital. Parents are Brian and Molly Fitzwilliam. The father, Brian, is serving his second term as a US Senator, and the family, with the exception of Kevin, reside in Alexandria, Virginia.

"Kevin Fitzwilliam entered the Republic of Ireland fifteen days ago as a tourist. At time of entry, he stated he planned to remain for one month. He has a return flight booked on Delta Airlines in sixteen days. He is listed as traveling alone. His flight was paid for with an American Express credit card registered to Kevin. He has had the card for the past thirteen months. The card has been paid on time every month. His flight reservations were made fifty-seven days in advance.

"Initial reports suggest the parents did not know he was traveling anywhere, let alone outside the US. We'll confirm that upon their arrival. Kevin resides in a Jefferson City apartment with two other friends, both males, both still in Jefferson City. All three attend the same private grammar school in Jefferson City, and the families have known one another for at least twenty-five years. Brian and Molly Fitzwilliam will be arriving tomorrow morning at 8:20 AM on Delta flight 1016. Embassy staff will be meeting them at the airport." When he'd finished, he looked up at the group, and asked, "Questions?"

"Where was he staying?" Suel asked.

"It's not clear at this time."

"Was there a cell phone in his possession?" Bergman asked.

"No," McCabe said. "He had his passport, with the father's business card attached and a twenty-euro note in his pocket. No wallet, no cellphone. A bit unusual for that age, no cellphone."

"Maybe he gave it to a friend or lost it. No wallet and cellphone suggests to me they might be sitting on a dresser top or a bed somewhere nearby. Twenty euros in his pocket, was he just out to grab lunch? And what is he doing here as a tourist? Visiting friends, maybe a girlfriend?" Suel said.

Bergman shrugged and said, "At this stage, all of the above."

"We located images from CCTV cameras. He entered Dame Lane at approximately twelve-forty-three PM. He entered via Trinity Street. He was alone, at least on the images we've located thus far. The closest college is Trinity. You can almost see the place from there. From your details, I take it he wasn't enrolled?" Suel said.

"He was not to our knowledge." Bergman flipped a page in the document he held, scanned down the page for a moment, then said, "He completed three semesters at Columbia College in Jefferson City, then dropped out in 2013. No record of any gainful employment over the last three years."

"I wonder what he was living on?" Crowley asked, more to himself than the room.

"Parents, maybe, or maybe he was doing odd jobs, someone that age he could do physical labor, take the payment in cash and stay off the books," Crowley said.

"Drugs?" Dillon asked.

"He comes from a fairly stable background," Bergman said. "His father is fairly solid in the Republican party."

"Wouldn't be the first time some senator's kid went off the reservation. I'm just suggesting we not discount it, although if that were his intent, Amsterdam, London or Marseilles would seem a better option," Dillon said.

"Or Mexico, it's closer to home, and he could get there for a lot less, but then why not just stay at home or drive over to Kansas City? I'm hoping we can get the answers to those questions tomorrow morning with the arrival of the parents," Bergman said.

"No arrest record?" Dillon asked.

"None that we're aware of. Not so much as a parking ticket."

"Anything in terms of a health problem, diabetes, mental illness, drug abuse?"

"Based on the records we've been able to access, he appears to have been a clean kid with no medical problems. He did play on the high school soccer team, which suggests some semblance of physical conditioning."

"So he's here for a month. Does not seem to be doing the tourist thing, traveling around the country. He has cash in his pocket, and he's walking around without a wallet and phone in his possession. That may suggest he was residing nearby, possibly Trinity based on his age," Crowley said.

"Dame Lane, coming off Trinity Street, that might suggest a familiarity with the place. He didn't seem to even glance at a couple posing for a selfie. Trinity Street is far more interesting than Dame Lane at that corner, so maybe he'd been there before, knew where he was going," Suel said.

"A lot of questions, and we need them answered as soon as possible," McCabe said, then drummed his fingers on the desk.

Suel's cellphone suddenly rang to the sound of some funeral dirge. "Hello. Yes, anything that…." He glanced at his watch. "I'll be there. No, no, we won't forget. Appreciate the call," he said and hung up.

"That was Doctor Byrne, the pathologist. She'll be finishing up in an hour and can give us a verbal report— small-caliber round to the heart. The round has been recovered. She'll be sending samples out for lab tests. We should have the results in a few days. No sign of intravenous drug use. No bruising on the body except for that which is consistent with his collapse once he was shot."

"All right. Let's make sure you're up there within the hour. I want us to stay on her good side, she's been a big help today. Until then, let's continue reviewing the CCTV tapes. Crowley, if you would check with Trinity just in case they have some listing of Fitzwilliam. It might be a good idea to get a list of current American students as well as where they're from in the States, see if there is any initial correlation. We'll want to interview them, see if this lad rings any bells. Agent Bergman, you are more than welcome to accompany DI Suel to the morgue if you so desire. Dillon, I'd like you along as well."

Dillon nodded and stood along with Crowley and Suel, they all filed out of the room. Special Agent Eric Bergman remained seated.

NINE

As they walked out to the parking, lot Suel said, "I'll drive." Once they stepped outside of the building, Bergman took a quick glance around, then said, "So, I hear you ran into some heat out at the airport earlier this year."

Dillon sort of shrugged, but didn't say anything.

"The Dildo saved two of our people. A right bollocks it was and would have been a hell of a lot worse if he hadn't been there. The bastards. So what's your background, Bergman?"

"Me? Did a couple of tours with the Army in Iraq, went back to school and got a Masters in international law. This is actually my first posting with the Diplomatic Security Service."

"How's it going?"

"Like everything else, good days and bad days. I'm currently the young kid on the block, and as you may know, shit has a tendency to flow downhill."

"Don't we know," Dillon said.

They drove up to the north side. Along the way, they stopped at a wine store on Ballymun called the Grape

Vine, not too far from the morgue. Dillon ran in and purchased two bottles of red wine and was back out in under three minutes.

Once Suel parked on Griffith Ave, he turned in his seat and said, "Dr. Byrne is the pathologist who performed the autopsy. She's good, but she's not going to have any answers regarding alcohol or drugs in the system. She's also working late, and once we leave, she's going to be working even later, so let's remember to cut her some slack. You can grab the wine bottles, Bergman, that'll put you forever in her good favor." With that, they went through the gate and up to the front door, where they rang the after-hours bell. Someone Suel apparently knew and referred to as Jimmy answered a few minutes later and let them in.

"Sad state of affairs, this mess. Doctor Byrne's in her office, working up that preliminary report," Jimmy said as he led them down the hallway toward Byrne's office. "Go ahead and knock, Paddy. You need anything I'll be in the lab, just give a yell."

Suel knocked on the door, then opened it just as Byrne called, "It's open."

She was dressed in blue scrubs and had her back to the door. She was typing on her computer as they entered. It looked like some sort of standard form up on her computer screen, and she appeared to be filling in a series of blanks and checking boxes. She glanced over her shoulder and smiled as Suel stepped into the office.

"Perfect timing. Take a seat. I'll have a copy ready for you in a couple of minutes."

"Doctor Byrne, this is Special Agent Eric Bergman with the American Embassy," Suel said.

Byrne removed her glasses, stood, and extended her hand. "Nice to meet you, Agent Bergman. Sorry it's under these circumstances."

"The pleasure is all mine. I appreciate you going the extra mile and working late. I hope you don't mind, I picked up some wine for you. Just a small token of the Embassy's appreciation."

Dillon and Suel got a shocked look on their face, and Byrne visibly bit her lip to stop from laughing. "Thank you so much," she said, taking the bottles from Bergman.

"Bloody hell," Suel said.

She placed the bottles on the floor in a corner next to the far side of her desk. "Nice to know someone has manners. You two plonkers still owe me. Have a seat Agent Bergman. Dillon and Suel can fight over the other chair. Let me just print this off. Three copies?"

"Do four, if you would please, McCabe will want one," Suel said as he slid into the other open chair. Dillon gave a sigh and leaned back against the wall.

Byrne made a couple of clicks with her mouse, then turned to face them in her chair just as the printer started up. "No real surprises, just confirmation of what we already suspected. The victim, Kevin Brian Fitzwilliam, has a height of five feet eleven inches. Weight 10.92

stone, that's 153 pounds. Cause of death is a small-caliber round, weight of just 85 grams. Maximum penetration is 6.5 inches based on standard charts. That's not a lot, but unfortunately enough to do this job.

"From what I determined from the trajectory, the victim appears to have been reaching up over his head with his right arm. Gunpowder residue on clothing and stippling on the body is consistent with the weapon at no more than an inch or two away when fired. At the exact moment he reached up, someone placed a small weapon literally into his armpit and fired. It was a freak shot. The downward trajectory passed through both lungs and struck the heart. Death occurred almost instantly, certainly before he hit the ground. I've recovered the round and have it logged in. Tissue samples were sent to the lab late this afternoon. Under the circumstances, we should be getting some results within twenty-four hours. One somewhat unique characteristic, the fingertips on both hands were calloused, the left hand more so than the right."

"Calloused fingertips?" Dillon said.

"I'd say he was a musician, a stringed instrument, guitar if I had to hazard a guess," Byrne said.

"What the hell would he be reaching for?" Suel said.

"Maybe he wasn't reaching. Maybe he was waving or giving someone a high-five. Could he have been falling and had extended his arm to break the fall? Maybe the shooter tripped him," Dillon said.

"Two attackers, one of them raises his arms?" Bergman said.

"I guess that's for you lot to figure out," Byrne replied. The printer had stopped, and she spun around on her chair, then reached below her desk and came up with a stack of papers. She counted off six sheets, stapled them together, then repeated the procedure three more times and handed the stack across her desk to Suel.

"Thanks for taking the time, Alicia," Suel said.

"Yeah, thank you," Dillon said.

"Nice meeting you, Doctor Byrne. Thank you," Bergman said.

"Please, call me Alicia. Best of luck, gentlemen. Let's hope you find whoever did this. Oh, one other thing I neglected to mention. The victim had a recent tattoo on his left bicep."

"Someone's name?" Dillon asked.

"Not exactly, it said 'U2'."

"U2? You mean like that knacker Bono and his band?" Suel said.

"Exactly. Red ink. I'd estimate application maybe sixty to ninety days ago."

"So now we just have to look for suspects who don't like U2," Dillon said.

"Best get started, going to be a late night for all of us," Suel said and pulled the office door open.

TEN

Suel climbed behind the wheel, started the car, then waited for three cars to pass before he made a U-turn and headed back the way they'd come. He turned onto Ballymun Road and drove past the Grape Vine where Dillon had purchased the bottles of wine earlier. They were headed in the general direction of Dillon's house, a mere half-mile away.

"Where are you going?" Dillon asked.

"There's a Macari's just up at the shops on the corner. Thought it might be best to grab a takeout. We're going to be searching through a few hours of CCTV footage, and God only knows what McCabe has lined up for us over the past hour. Bound to be a late night."

They pulled into a parking place a moment after a woman backed out, parking directly in front of the door to Macari's. The front of the building was white with large windows. All three of them climbed out of the car and entered the shop. Dillon was in the lead. A line of a half-dozen people stood at the counter.

"What can I get you?" a girl behind the counter asked. She was dark-haired with bright blue eyes. Her hair was pulled back in a sort of bun, and she wore a white apron along with a baseball cap labeled "Macari's" in red letters.

"Fish and chips, and a Coke," Suel said.

"I'll have the same," Dillon said, then looked over at Bergman. "He's paying."

"Yeah, your man's paying for me, too," Suel said.

Bergman looked at the two of them, then nodded. "I'd better, or they'll run out of here with their order, and you'd have to call the Guards. I'll have the pulled pork and chips," he said.

"I take back some of the things your mates have been saying about you, Bergman," Suel said, and then all three of them laughed. They carried their bags of food back to the car. Suel reversed out of the parking place and headed back to the office.

Once in the office, Dillon and Bergman spread their meals out on a table in the break room. Suel joined them a moment later after depositing the initial autopsy report from Alicia Byrne on McCabe's desk.

No one spoke for a minute or two as they started in on their meals. Dillon finally broke the silence. "I'm thinking about the calloused fingertips and the tattoo."

"U2," Bergman said through a mouth of pulled pork and chewed.

"Bono," Suel scoffed and took a large bite of fish.

"Didn't they start by playing gigs on Grafton Street?" Dillon said.

Suel took a large swig from his Coke bottle, appeared to stifle a belch, and then said, "Maybe, that's one of the many rumors. They were known as The Hype at one time. I actually went to a gig they played back in the late 70s. They changed their name to U2 and won some contest, I think in Limerick. Along with the money, something like five hundred quid, they got a recording contract, cut a record that did okay in Ireland, and the rest, as they say, is history."

"So, Kevin Fitzwilliam has enough of a thing for U2 that he gets the name tattooed on his arm. He's wearing a U2 t-shirt when he's murdered, and he's playing enough music, guitar, again I'm guessing, that his fingers are heavily calloused. Just a thought here, but what if he came to Ireland in an effort to copy U2's success? What if he was somehow picking up guitar gigs with a band or at least some other musicians? Maybe he's playing at pubs or even on a corner with a tip jar. That might account for spending money here. Maybe he was playing gigs at home, and that's how he made his money. He was working, probably hard, but it was all off the books."

"So he leaves the gigantic US market and comes over here to little old Ireland to find his fame and fortune?" Suel said. He took a bite out of one of his chips and shook his head. "Doesn't seem to make any sense, the whole idea sounds a bit daft."

"Yeah, but I can see some twenty-three-year-old kid doing just that," Bergman said.

"You wouldn't happen to have contact information for his roommates, would you?" Dillon asked.

Bergman set his pulled pork sandwich down on the styrofoam tray and took out his cellphone. "Let me make a call. I think I can probably get the number if they've got a landline. The cellphone numbers might take a little longer." He looked at his watch and said, "It's just early afternoon over there in Missouri right now, let me try and reach the roommates."

ELEVEN

At no surprise, there wasn't a landline number for the apartment Kevin Fitzwilliam shared with two friends. Suel was back reviewing CCTV images. Bergman was off doing something, possibly making more phone calls back to the States in an effort to garner any additional information on Kevin Fitzwilliam. Dillon was online, doing a search on designer jeans. When he clicked on the Nordstrom's site, the exact pair of jeans Kevin Fitzwilliam had been wearing showed up on the screen, black, with bleach stains and two areas on the upper left thigh that looked to be patched.

"Suel, come on over and check this out. I found the jeans Fitzwilliam was wearing. Here, check this out," he said as Suel stepped over to his desk. "Looks like the same bleached areas, the torn and patched upper thigh, an exact copy."

"You're shitting me, four hundred and fifty-five dollars. For a pair of torn jeans? God, I am so out of touch."

"Certainly not cheap, and then the t-shirt."

"U-2."

"Probably forty bucks at a concert."

Bergman was suddenly looking over their shoulders. "That's what he was wearing, Fitzwilliam?"

"Yeah," Suel said. "Four hundred and fifty-five US dollars. For fecks sake, I've had cars that didn't cost that much. Then the U2 t-shirt, add another forty dollars for that. Certainly sounds like a lot of disposable income for a lad. Maybe we should check and see when was the last time U2 toured the US."

"They've toured the States every year since at least 1980," Bergman said.

"You're shitting me. How in the hell do you know that?" Suel asked.

Bergman shrugged and said, "What can I tell you? I'm a fan." At that moment, his cellphone rang. He pulled it out of a front pocket, looked at the caller ID, then said, "Oh, that was fast. Hello. Yes, yes, I did." He reached over and picked up a pen from Dillon's desk, turned over a sheet of paper, and said, "Okay, go ahead. Yeah. Okay. Got it, great. You wouldn't happen to have an age on either one, would you? Yeah, no, that makes sense. Okay, thank you very much, appreciate the speedy service. Yes, you do the same. Thanks again."

"Something positive?" Dillon asked.

"Name and cellphone numbers of the two roommates. Since their presence in Jefferson City has been confirmed, I'm going to presume they've been informed of Kevin Fitzwilliam's death." Bergman glanced at his watch. It was just after ten PM in Dublin. They were the only people in the office. "I'm going to try and reach them. It's just a little after four back in Missouri. With any luck, we can reach at least one of them." He input one of the phone numbers, then set the phone down on Dillon's desk and put it on speaker.

It rang four times before a questioning voice answered, "Hello?"

Bergman glanced at his note on the sheet of paper and said, "I'd like to speak to Joshua Hughes."

"Speaking."

"Joshua, my name is Eric Bergman. I'm a Special Agent with the American Embassy in Dublin, Ireland."

"This is about Kevin, isn't it?"

"Yes, it is. I've got you on speakerphone. I'm with US Marshal Jack Dillon—"

"Hello, Joshua," Dillon said.

"You can call me Josh, everyone does."

"Detective Inspector Patrick Suel with the Dublin Police is with us also."

"Good evening, Josh."

"Hello."

"Listen, Josh, we're trying to get as much background information as we can on Kevin. His parents will be arriving in Dublin tomorrow morning. Can you help us?"

"I can try. Jake and I have been sitting here ever since we got the word and…."

"Is that Jacob Schmidt, your roommate?"

"Yes, sir."

"Hello, Jacob."

"Hello, sir. We don't know much about what happened except that Kevin was killed. Was it a car accident?"

Bergman glanced up at Suel and Dillon, Suel shook his head.

"I don't have that information," Bergman said. "We're hoping you can fill us in on Kevin, what he was like, what he did, was he visiting anyone over here, that sort of thing."

"This is Jake, sir. He was a really nice guy. He loved telling jokes, and of course, playing his guitar."

"And his singing, he was with two bands here, and a third group was trying to get him to join them."

"I'm not sure if he knew anyone over there. He rented a room at some bed and breakfast place lined up for the first couple of days, and then he was just gonna go by the seat of his pants and see what turned up."

"Was he planning to travel the country?" Dillon asked.

"No, he was hoping to get all his gigs right in Dublin."

"Gigs?"

"Yeah, for his guitar playing and singing. He figured if he had time in Dublin, playing with some band and singing, you know, it would look good when he tried to get an agent. He could tell folks he'd been international."

"Where did he get the Dublin idea?" Suel asked.

"U2," both voices chimed in.

"He was a fanatic, knew all about them, figured he could just follow their path forty years later."

"Even got a U2 tattoo. Course, he didn't tell his folks."

"Did he get on with his folks?" Bergman asked.

"Yeah. He and his dad went at it a couple years back, but that was 'cause Kevin dropped out of school, and his dad was worried he didn't have a plan."

"Yeah. Actually, he had a plan, his dad just didn't like it. The guy is kind of a control freak. Then a couple years ago they came to some sort of agreement. His dad said Kevin could try the music thing, and if it wasn't happening after thirty-six months, he would have to en-roll back in school."

"You know when the thirty-six months is up?" Dillon asked.

"First of the year," they both said.

"He was really aware of it. That was one of the big pushes to try and get things moving in Dublin. Kevin figured he could be the second coming of U2. Even had the cover laid out for his first album. The sun coming up over some shot of the Liffey River. It actually looked kind of cool."

"Have you talked to him since he came to Dublin?" Suel asked.

"We didn't actually talk with him. We sent a couple of emails back and forth, but nothing for maybe the last week."

"Yeah, I think it was last Sunday. That was the one where he'd played the night before, said there was this hot chick with the band he was singing with."

"Yeah, he'd done a gig with some band, and they seemed to like what he brought to the group."

"Plus, this chick was making a pass at him."

Whichever one was in the background laughed at that last comment.

"Did he have a girlfriend?" Dillon asked.

"No. Not that there weren't some always trying."

"Yeah, Angie and that Debbie, remember?"

"He always said they'd take too much time, and he wanted to become a star first. Figured he could pick and choose after that."

"What about drugs?" Bergman asked.

"With Kevin? No way. He was the last person who'd ever do drugs. He figured if he led a clean life, he would just become a star that much faster. No, no drugs. He was good for maybe one beer over the course of a night. He'd have a glass of hot water and honey…."

"With a fresh lemon."

"…before he played a gig, said it helped make his voice just that much better."

"He sounds like he was a pretty straight arrow," Dillon said.

"That goes without saying. More than once, he was our designated driver."

"He have any problems with anyone, someone maybe jealous of him?"

"You mean someone who'd want to hurt him? No, he was a really nice guy. I mean, a little boring, he'd practice all day and…."

"Yeah, really religious about the practicing. God, he'd be in his bedroom hour after hour, going over and over the same shit. Course, that's what made him so good. I mean, he really worked at it."

"Did he have an agent or anyone to handle the business side of things?" Dillon asked.

"No. There was someone last spring, and Kevin got all pumped about that, but it kind of fizzled out."

"Yeah, the guy wanted him to move up to Chicago, and then he wanted lifetime rights or something to everything Kevin had written. Anyway, it didn't work out, and that's kind of when he started thinking about doing the U2 thing."

"Were his parents aware he was traveling to Ireland?"

There was a long pause. "No, sir."

"We spoke to them this morning. His mom was really upset, as you can imagine."

"Yeah, and his dad was really pissed off. He was yelling on the phone."

"And you don't know the name of the band he played with over here or where they played?"

"No, he just said he made a hundred bucks…."

"Euros."

"Oh yeah, a hundred euros, and that they really liked him. Said he was heading out to practice with them. The email was only a couple of lines long said he'd get back to us, then the next thing we heard was the call we got from his folks this morning."

"Any more questions?" Bergman asked after a brief silence.

Dillon and Suel shook their heads.

"Okay, guys. We appreciate your help. I'm sorry it's under these circumstances. We may be back to you with a question or two, just trying to get things sorted out over here."

"Is it all right if we tell our friends? We weren't sure if we could."

Bergman looked at Dillon, who nodded. "Yeah, I suppose that would be all right. Ummm, maybe try and check with Kevin's parents. They're still in the US. I'd guess for a couple more hours before they board the plane to come over here. Just make sure it's okay with them. They obviously have a lot on their plate right now."

"Okay. Please let us know when you have more information," one of the guys said. It sounded like Josh, but the voices were pretty similar and it was tough to tell them apart. "Ummm, thanks," he said, but then his voice started cracking, sounding like he was about to cry, and he disconnected.

"Fecking U2," Suel said.

"Sounds like the kid came over here to find fame and fortune," Bergman said.

"We need to find that band he played with last weekend. That's our starting point."

"The fact that they gave him a hundred quid, if indeed they did, that's not some kids playing on a street corner, they were booked somewhere, in a club or a pub, or Christ, maybe even playing a wedding reception or something," Suel said.

"Maybe it was The Stag's Head or someplace near there."

"Temple Bar district's as good a place as any to start," Suel said and looked at his watch. "We get down there tonight, we'd still have maybe two hours to check places out. If we split up, the three of us could cover a lot of ground in two hours."

TWELVE

Dillon was up on Dame Lane, walking into places asking the manager or bar staff if they recognized the black and white image he had of Kevin Fitzwilliam. No one recognized the photo in The Stag's Head or the Dame Tavern. He backtracked and stopped in at the Bankers Lounge, Keough's, The International, and a half-dozen other pubs and came up empty each and every time.

Suel and Bergman were down in the Temple Bar area, going from pub to pub. Bergman started at the Palace Bar, and Suel started at the opposite end at the Porterhouse, both of them working their way toward the Temple Bar Square, where all three planned to meet up.

It was close to one when Dillon spotted Bergman coming out of the Temple Bar Pub. He and Bergman had chatted for just a brief moment when they saw Suel exiting The Quays and heading toward them.

"Any luck?" Dillon asked.

"Nothing but a big blank. No one recognized the picture, and no one picked up on his name. Tell you the truth, there are so many tourists going through here all day, every day, it would be damn near impossible for them to remember some kid they may have seen once or twice. One of them told me they get stopped fifty times a day by someone asking if they can play a couple of tunes. He said the few they do let play are usually absolute shite."

"Did you say U2 used to play on Grafton Street?" Dillon asked.

"That's the legend, but to my knowledge, it's never been documented, and by the late 70's they were already making a name for themselves and wouldn't have to stoop to being buskers on the street. But there are a couple of pubs up there that might be worth talking to." Suel glanced at his watch. "Too late for it now. They've got the statue of Phil Lynott up there and…."

"Who the hell is Phil Lynott?"

"Iconic guitar player with Thin Lizzie, first black Irishman to make it big."

"Got it. Is there any place that U2 would be associated with?"

"Used to be the Clarence Hotel, just down the lane and around the corner from here," Suel said. "Relax, I already checked in there. No one knew a thing. Place used to be owned by Bono and The Edge, but Christ, they sold it to some investment group or something, sometime back in the nineties, I think. Look, lads, it's a little after one. I say we get some sleep and start hitting it early tomorrow morning. Be in the office at eight?"

Dillon nodded and yawned.

"You gonna join us?" Suel asked Bergman.

"Yeah, I think so, unless they want me at the initial meeting with the Fitzwilliams in the morning."

"Oh yeah, that's right. What do you think the odds are for all of us attending that?"

"Pretty good. You might want to check with DCI McCabe first. Then the other thing is that they'll just be arriving. I don't know, a five or six-hour flight, all they're dealing with, not to mention the time change, they may want to just hit the sack first," Bergman said.

"Keep us posted. That meeting would obviously take precedence. I'd say they'll want to be brought up to speed on the investigation thus far. If those two kids earlier on the phone are to be believed, the Senator will probably want up-to-date information as to what, where, and how we're doing things," Suel said.

"Can you blame him?" Dillon said. "I sure as hell wouldn't want to trade places with them."

"Let's the two of us plan on meeting in the office and touching base before we do anything," Suel said.

THIRTEEN

Suel drove them back to the office, where they climbed into their respective vehicles and headed home. Dillon pulled into his parking area in the front garden and climbed out of his car. He heard scratching from inside the front door almost immediately. Lucifer.

He unlocked the front door, and Lucifer scrambled past him, then circled a couple of times and squatted. He seemed to have a smile on his face, and he stared back at Dillon.

"Good boy, Lucifer," Dillon said, then waited until he had finished and walked back into the house. Things inside looked in fairly good shape. The wastebasket in the kitchen had been knocked over, and an empty package of ground beef chewed up and scattered around the kitchen floor. There was a pillow from the living room couch over in the corner of the sitting room, but it didn't appear to be in too bad a shape. Upstairs, the pillow on the bed was still warm from where Lucifer must have been sleeping when Dillon pulled in.

He really didn't care. He dropped his clothes on the floor, climbed into bed, and immediately fell asleep. Lucifer curled up on the pillow next to him.

Dillon's phone woke him just a little after six.

"Hello," he groaned.

"Oh, sorry, did I wake you?" Suel said.

"No. It was time to get up, get dressed, and go home anyway."

Suel paused for a moment. "Can you get into the office in the next hour? I'm thinking of crawling through the CCTV tapes of Grafton Street. With the two of us going through them, we could get a good portion of them reviewed before the meeting with the parents. Be nice to have that under our belts. I'm afraid at this stage all we might have for them is a laundry list of things we've eliminated."

"An hour, yeah, I can be there."

"See you then. I'll bring a sweet," Suel said and hung up.

Dillon let Lucifer sleep. He took a hot shower, made coffee, dressed, ate a piece of toast, then had to shake Lucifer awake and coax him outside with a milk bone. When he finished, he let him back in the house, cleaned up his deposits outside from the past two days, then drove to the office.

Suel was already at his desk when Dillon arrived. He was scanning through a CCTV tape and, without looking up, said, "Got us some doughnuts, in the bag." He indicated a white paper bag on the edge of his desk with a turn of his head. What appeared to be a half-eaten glazed doughnut rested next to his keyboard. He handed another list of CCTV tapes to Dillon and said, "Burn a copy and just like before, you start at the bottom and work your way up. We'll meet in the middle."

Dillon opened the paper bag, grabbed two dough-nuts, and dropped them at his desk. He made a copy of the list of CCTV tapes, dropped the original back on Suel's desk, then settled in front of his computer. He took a bite of a doughnut and started working his way through the first tape.

It had been a little over an hour. Dillon had gone through both doughnuts and three cups of coffee that tasted like they'd been on the burner for the past three days when Suel called out.

"Jack, I think I got something here. Come 'mere to me now and check this out."

Dillon hurried over to his desk and looked at the im-age. It was definitely Kevin Fitzwilliam, wearing the same clothes he had on when he was shot.

"When was this?" Dillon asked.

"Three days ago. The lad seems to be headed to a destination instead of just wandering."

"Plus, he's got that guitar case. Maybe he's going to meet up with the band he bragged about."

"Maybe. Although it's just after the noon hour. Bit early for a band."

They watched for four more images before he disappeared from the camera. Suel printed off all five images, then logged onto the next tape. There he was again, this time just three images, but it was Fitzwilliam carrying his guitar case and heading up Grafton Street toward Stephen's Green. Suel printed off the images again and logged onto the next tape.

There was Kevin Fitzwilliam again. Only this time, he'd stopped and was opening his guitar case. Farther up Grafton Street was a man standing next to a sand sculpture of a sleeping dog.

Fitzwilliam began playing, and on every image, the crowd had clearly grown, lots of smiling people. As Suel moved from image to image, he printed off a copy. There were four or five minutes' worth of images, and then someone approached Fitzwilliam, and there was a conversation of some sort that did not seem to be going the young man's way. In short order, he packed up his guitar, left, and the crowd dispersed.

"I wonder what that was about?"

"I'm guessing he just showed up and started playing."

"Yeah?"

"You actually need a permit to be playing there. I think you can only play for an hour, but they require you to start and stop at the top of the hour. He might have had a visitor's permit, that would seem logical, but you'd have to know it was required before you'd get one. That was probably someone from the Business Association or the County Council who just happened to come along and shut him down."

"You recognize him?"

"No, but I can send the image over to both offices and see if someone does. It's a start. I'll get on it now."

Dillon's phone rang. Bergman.

"Hello?"

"Hi, Marshal, Jack Bergman. We're about to escort Senator and Mrs. Fitzwilliam to the Embassy. We'll give them an hour to get cleaned up, but they'd like to meet as soon as possible."

"Okay, we'll be at the Embassy in an hour and…."

"We're just leaving the airport now. Make it an hour and a half. Ask for me at the desk. I'll alert them you'll be coming in. Will Suel be coming?"

"Yeah, and I suspect McCabe, although we haven't seen him yet this morning. We got some more images of Kevin Fitzwilliam on CCTV."

"That's better than us coming up empty-handed down in Temple Bar last night. I'll alert reception at the Embassy. See you then," Bergman said and disconnected.

"News?" Suel asked.

"Only that we'll be meeting the parents in about an hour and a half. Have you seen McCabe yet?"

"No. Send him a text message. He's addicted to that damn phone. He'll get it."

FOURTEEN

The Chancery building of the United States Embassy in Dublin was a modern, circular building built in 1964. One of the ugliest buildings in Dublin, it was deemed "no longer suitable" in 2014 from the standpoint of size, security, and construction.

Suel and Dillon were headed toward the building when Dillon's phone rang. Bergman.

"Hello."

"Change in plans, we're at the Ambassador's residence in Phoenix Park, the Deerfield Residence. You know it?"

Dillon lifted his phone and asked Suel, "You know where the Deerfield residence is?"

"In Phoenix Park?"

"Yeah," Dillon said.

"I know it. We're headed in the wrong direction," Suel said, then put on his blinker and turned at the next corner.

"Yeah, Suel knows where it is."

"Pull up to the front. They'll be expecting you. I've left word at the front gate."

"See you shortly."

"You ever been there?" Suel asked once Dillon hung up the phone.

"No, never even seen the place," Dillon said.

"It'll be nice to see how the other half lives. I've been past it a million times, but never been inside."

"Stick with me, Paddy, I'll bring you up on the social ladder."

Suel gave him a long, disbelieving look.

They arrived fifteen minutes later, and after having their IDs checked by the Marine security detail at the front gate, a white, concrete affair with a center gate and two pedestrian gates on either side, they were waved through. They drove up the circular drive to the front entry. Another security detail waved them into a parking area, then escorted them to one of three cottages behind the residence. Bergman met them out in front of a cottage.

"Any trouble finding us?"

"No, I knew where it was, but first-time visitor. To be honest, I never knew these places existed," Suel said, indicating the structures behind the massive ambassador's residence.

"The cottages, yeah, they're nice. Gives folks a bit of privacy and a little better chance to relax from all the official routine. We'll be meeting with Senator Brian Fitzwilliam. I'm not sure his wife will be joining us. DCI McCabe is already inside. Questions?"

Both Dillon and Suel shook their head. Suel carried a briefcase containing the manila file folder with the images from the CCTV tapes as well as the autopsy report.

"Okay, let's get started," Bergman said, and headed off, Dillon and Suel followed closely behind. Suel hadn't been kidding when he said, *"How the other half lives."*

Bergman opened the door to a two-story, red-brick, victorian cottage with a red tile roof, cream-colored trim, and stepped inside. The entryway was paneled in a dark wood that looked two hundred years old. There was a fireplace with a wooden mantel and three trophies sitting on it. The trophies appeared more recent than the paneling, maybe just a hundred years old.

"McCabe and the Senator are in the library," Bergman said and walked down a dark-paneled hallway to a closed door. He knocked softly on the door, then opened it. "DI Patrick Suel and Marshal Jack Dillon," he said as he stepped into the room.

"Come in, come in," a voice boomed out. As they followed Bergman into the room, a man rose from a wingback chair. His neatly trimmed brown hair was greying at the temples. He was tanned, fit-looking, and wore dark blue trousers, a white shirt, and no tie. The sleeves on his shirt were rolled up on his forearms. His eyes were red-rimmed. A suit coat matching his trousers was draped across the back of a wooden chair standing over in the corner. McCabe sat opposite him on a couch, looking tired. He rose a moment after they entered. Dillon couldn't be sure, but he thought he might still be in yesterday's clothes.

"Gentlemen, thank you for coming and for your efforts thus far," the Senator said, then extended his hand to Suel. "Brian Fitzwilliam."

"My deepest condolences, sir," Suel said and shook hands.

Fitzwilliam nodded, then directed his attention toward Dillon. "And you must be the man I've been hearing about," Fitzwilliam said, extending his hand. He glanced toward McCabe as he made the comment, indicating the source.

"So sorry to be meeting you under these circumstances, sir."

Fitzwilliam nodded again, then indicated the couch and another chair. Suel settled in next to McCabe on the couch. Dillon sat in the chair. Fitzwilliam settled back into the wingback chair, then pulled it forward no more than an inch. Bergman grabbed a wooden chair from another corner and pulled it alongside Fitzwilliam.

Fitzwilliam gave a sigh, then opened a file on the coffee table in front of him. The file consisted of a stack of papers, and on top of the papers, maybe a dozen copies of the same 5x7 full-color photo of his son, Kevin, without the wisp of the beard. He handed a color photo to everyone, then picked up the sheaf of papers.

"These are a copy of the passport document information, finger-prints, blood type, that sort of thing. I guess under the circumstances, you probably already have most of this information." He paused for a moment and cleared his throat. "Listen, I hope you'll forgive Molly, but for right now, she's just unable to go through with this meeting. We've given her a sedative. She's upstairs sleeping, thank God. At least I hope she is. It's been difficult for her, for both of us actually," he said, and suddenly one lone tear ran down his left cheek. He cleared his throat and brushed the tear away.

"Please excuse me. I'm just a bit out of sorts myself. Okay, what can you tell me?"

"Kevin was killed by a small-caliber weapon, fired just beneath his right arm. Autopsy results conclude he died almost instantly and, a small consolation I realize, but he experienced no pain," McCabe said.

"Do we know who killed him?"

McCabe looked over at Suel.

"Not at this time. We do know a number of things and continue to put together more pieces of the puzzle. We know that he entered Dame Lane by himself at approximately 12:47 PM. He entered via Trinity Street. He remained by himself up until someone approached and fired the weapon. At this stage, we do not know who that individual is. We are leaning toward the idea of a recent acquaintance.

"We have no eyewitnesses, at least none who have come forward. We do know that Kevin was hoping to be discovered, that is, musically, and that he had recently emailed his roommates back in Mission City...."

"Josh and Jacob?"

"Yes, sir. We know he had emailed them a brief message stating that he'd participated in a performance with a group, had been paid the sum of one hundred euros, and they were asking him to join the group. At this stage, we do not know the name of the group, and we have been unable to corroborate that information. We only learned about it late last night."

"We have CCTV images of Kevin walking along Dame Lane moments before his murder. He is alone on all the images. We have images of him playing his guitar as a busker on Grafton Street the day prior to his murder."

"Busker?" Fitzwilliam said.

"A street performer, musicians, jugglers, singers, clowns. You have to obtain a license. Our images of Kevin performing suggest he didn't have a license, and he was asked to leave. My sense is he probably didn't realize you needed a license."

"Do you have those images with you, the ones on Grafton Street?"

Suel nodded and opened his file, paged toward the back, then pulled out a number of sheets of paper and handed them to Fitzwilliam. He paged through the images, slowly, just the hint of a smile on his face. When he'd finished, he cleared his throat and set the images on the coffee table.

"Jesus Christ, this is all just so God damned unreal."

Dillon, Suel, Bergman, and McCabe just sat quietly and waited.

"Molly will have a better handle on this. I don't know how many years he saved up for his guitar. He took a percentage from every gig he got paid for and finally had enough. Took him the better part of two years to save up the money. It's signed by Bono and some guy who goes by 'The Edge.' Jesus Christ. The damn thing cost him thousands. I was against it, of course, but I finally realized he had his sights set on it, and damned if he didn't work his ass off and accomplish the goal. Bought it from some dealer out in LA. My God, it took the place of a woman in his life. He'd play the thing hour after hour, had a special cloth he'd wipe it down with whenever he picked it up to play and whenever he was finished. None of us were allowed to touch it. We could only look at it. Had it insured for thousands." He paused for a long moment and stared off, most likely back in some distant time with his son. "Damn it," he said, then shook his head, which seemed to return him to the here and now, as awful as it was at the moment. "Okay, so where do you go from here?"

McCabe leaned forward and looked at Dillon and Suel.

FIFTEEN

Bergman was standing with Dillon and Suel next to their car in the parking area." Thoughts?" he asked.

"I wouldn't want to trade places with Fitzwilliam or his wife just now," Suel said.

"Yeah, she's just barely able to hold it together," Bergman said, then looked back toward the cottage and shook his head. "They'll be here until the body is released, then escort it back to the States. They've private transportation lined up."

Dillon gave him a questioning look.

"A donor, private jet of some sort. They'll be flown back to DC, pick up the rest of the family, then go on to Jefferson City. At this stage, things are still up in the air."

"I'm thinking, if we could get an image of the guitar the father mentioned, that might possibly be a motive if the thing has an actual value besides sentimental. Interesting comment that it took the place of a woman in his life, especially in conjunction with what we heard on the phone last night," Dillon said.

"Yeah, I'll see if we can get that. Where are you two off to now?"

"We'll be combing Grafton Street, start with the shops where he set up the other day. Maybe there's something there. I know it's slim," Suel said in response to Bergman's expression. "Right now, it's about all we got."

"That and just the fact that it seemed he might be crashing with someone in the immediate area. We could start looking at rentals," Dillon said.

"And vacant buildings. Maybe he was squatting somewhere. And that damn band that gave him the hundred quid, find them, we might start to get some real answers."

"Musicians Union?" Dillon said. "Maybe he contacted them, or they have a method of contacting members. Someone might have known him or know of that damn band."

"I've got a mate who's in the Union. Why the bloody hell didn't I think of it before? Hang on," Suel said, then pulled out his phone and hit a speed dial number.

"Desi, ya bollocks." Suel nodded at Bergman and Dillon. "Oh, I wish I could, but I'm working. Have a question for you, you still tight with the Musicians Union? Yeah, listen, did you hear about that young American shot on Dame Lane the other day? Yeah, that's the one. Turns out, he was over here hoping to be discovered like Bono and his lot. I know, I know, that's exactly what I thought, but here's the deal, we suspect he may have done a gig with a band, got paid a hundred quid and they maybe extended an invitation to join the band. No. I don't know. That's why I wanted to contact the Union, see if they might put out a blurb to members, maybe word it in a way that suggests they're always looking out for the rights of musicians, that sort of thing. They are? Liberty Hall, you say." Suel nodded again. "Yeah, course I can hold. Much appreciated, Desi."

He lifted the cellphone up and said, "He's getting the number for me. Thinks he might have a name, too. I'm thinking we might— Yeah, Desi. You will? Oh, that's great. Much appreciated. I owe you a pint," he said, then disconnected.

"He's going to text me the phone number and the name of someone at the Union office. I think we might head over there first. Liberty Hall, it's not too far from Temple Bar, just down a bit on the other side of the Liffey."

They left Bergman with the promise to touch base later in the day, then drove off to Liberty Hall and the MUI, Musicians' Union of Ireland.

Sixteen

Liberty Hall was on the Eden Quay near the Customs House in Dublin. It was a square sixteen-story building built in the early to mid 60s. At sixteen stories, it was the third tallest building in Ireland.

Suel parked the Garda vehicle in a no-parking zone alongside Liberty Hall, and they walked in. They took an elevator up to the Musicians' Union office.

As they opened the door, a paunchy, balding man with a thin grey ponytail was just walking back to an office. He was dipping a tea bag into a steaming mug, stopped, and said, "Can I help you?"

"Yeah," Suel said. "I spoke to a Joe Carroll just a few minutes ago. I—"

"Oh, you're the Guards. That was fast. This is about the American killed over in Dame Lane the other day?"

Suel nodded.

"I'm Joe Carroll. Nice to meet you. Not sure how I can help you, but come on back to the office. Care for a cuppa?"

"No thanks and this bollocks is American and hasn't developed the culture yet to enjoy the beverage."

Carroll smiled at that and said, "Just more for the rest of us. Come on back." He led the way down a short hall and into an office about the size of a small bathroom stall. A couple of black and white images were framed and hanging on the wall, presumably a much younger, thinner Joe Carroll with a full head of long, dark hair. In the photo, he held a guitar and was surrounded by a half-dozen people Dillon didn't recognize.

"Grab a seat, there," he said, stepping round to the far side of a file-covered desk. "I did a quick check on your man's name, Kevin Fitzwilliam?"

"Right," Suel said.

"Yeah, drew a complete blank. If he knew about us, he didn't bother to contact from what I could tell. That said, it sounds like he was here just a short time."

"Two weeks," Dillon said.

"Yeah, so under the circumstances, it wouldn't be out of line to not contact us. Honestly, how old did you say he was?"

"Twenty-three."

"That age, they all think they have a better idea of how to make the big time. Save paying our membership dues and maybe use the funds for a better purpose, like getting their girlfriends plastered and into bed. They all need to have life shoved up their ass a few times, have the check bounce, or not get paid at all. After that happens, we start to make a little more sense to them."

"He told some friends back in the States he did a couple of numbers with a band. They paid him a hundred quid and wanted him to join their band. That sound reasonable to you?" Suel asked.

Carroll leaned back in his chair and seemed to think about that for a long moment. "People are always moving from one group to another. A lot of our members are in more than one group. So, doing a set with a group and being asked to join them, that's not out of the ordinary. Making a hundred quid, that suggests they really liked him, or the other thought could be they knew of him, and he was paid to be with them. You know, the payment was arranged in advance. Maybe they heard about him, wanted to get him before anyone else did. A hundred quid to someone just starting out can be a pretty big incentive."

"Anyway, we're trying to find out what band it was that paid him. Kid wanted to be the next Bono, was really into U2. Had a guitar he purchased for over two grand that belonged to The Edge. I guess the thing was autographed by Bono and The Edge," Dillon said.

"We were hoping you'd consider sending an email out to members, telling them a musician was murdered, maybe even say he wasn't a member, but the wellbeing of all musicians is a Union concern, that sort of thing, and ask for help in identifying the band," Suel said.

"You're thinking someone in that group would have killed him?"

"No, not at all. But they may be able to give us some information. Right now, we know he was in Dublin because we have a body, and that's about all we know. Be nice to learn if he was staying with someone, otherwise we're really grabbing at straws at this point. This shooting doesn't appear to be random. What if we got some nutcase out there who wants to kill guitar players?" Dillon said.

Carroll took a sip from his tea mug, then drummed his fingers on the desk for a moment. "Tell you what, you get me a picture of your man and maybe one of that guitar as well, I'll get something out to the members. Can't promise you anything, but we won't know till we try."

Suel opened the file he carried and pulled out the color image of Kevin Fitzwilliam they'd received barely an hour ago. "I can let you have this if I can get it back. Let me make a phone call and see about a shot of that guitar."

"Nice-looking kid," Carroll said, studying the photo. "I'll just scan this, and you can leave with it." He opened a desk drawer and handed a business card to Suel. "Make your call on the guitar image and have them send it to my email address there on the card. I'll be back in just a minute."

Suel checked his phone call log and tapped on a number. Bergman answered on the second ring. They had a quick conversation. Bergman was still at the cottage and promised to see if he could get an image of the guitar. He also suggested Suel contact Jacob Schmidt and Joshua Hughes, Kevin's roommates in Jefferson

City, and see if they had any images of the guitar they could email.

Suel called Josh Hughes next. At just a little past one in the afternoon in Dublin, it would be a little after seven in the morning back in Missouri.

"Josh Hughes?" Suel said just as Carroll stepped back into the office and placed the photo of Kevin Fitzwilliam in front of Suel.

"Josh, this is Detective Inspector Patrick Suel, with the Dublin Police. We spoke earlier. Yes. No, not as of yet. Listen, I'm calling to see if either you or Jacob would have some pictures of Kevin with his guitar or the guitar all by itself. You do? Wonderful. Let me give you a couple of email addresses, and if you could get those off to us as quickly as possible, that would be a big help. Yes. Yes, this morning. We met with his father. Okay, really appreciate the help," he said, then gave Carroll's email address along with his own. "Thanks, Josh. Yeah, as soon as we learn something, we'll be in touch. Right."

"They have some images?" Dillon asked once Suel hung up.

"A number of images with the lad playing his guitar. They weren't too sure about a shot of just the guitar, but it's a start. They'll be sending them your way," he said to Carroll. "I'm thinking if you could put my number in your email, you know for a contact point, it would save you the problem of fielding calls," he said and handed his business card across the desk to Carroll.

Dillon dug his card out of his wallet and did the same.

"Let me get going on this email. Soon as I get the images of the instrument, I'll get it out there, and we'll see what happens," Carroll said.

"Really appreciate the help," Dillon said.

"Hey, some bastard attacked a musician. That's not on."

SEVENTEEN

As Suel pulled away from the curb he said, "Let's head over to Grafton Street. I want to talk to the shop owners where the kid was playing, see if anyone can tell us anything. Then back to the office and we can check the statements from people who said they heard the shot fired."

"You think we'll get any action from Carroll's email?" Dillon said.

"The email? I think it can't hurt, and God, but we need something to break loose on this. We're in day two, and we got squat right now."

They were waiting for the light to change before they took the Sean O'Casey Bridge over the Liffey and headed to Grafton Street when Dillon's phone rang. Bergman.

"Yeah, Eric," Dillon answered.

"You into something right now?"

"Just finished up with Joe Carroll at the Musicians' Union. He's going to send an email to members asking for any information on the band that supposedly paid Fitzwilliam. We're headed over to Grafton Street to talk—"

"Would you have time to meet with the Fitzwill-iams? Mrs. Fitzwilliam is up and expressed a desire to meet with you."

"Now?"

"Well, the sooner the better, but if you're into some-thing, I can cover for you, and we'll do it another time."

"Hang on," Dillon said, then turned to Suel. "Mrs. Fitzwilliam wants to meet with us. I'll leave it up to you."

"She's up? I thought they had her sedated?"

"Well, she's up, apparently. I don't know, if we—"

"Maybe she has something. Maybe the son con-tacted her and the father doesn't know. Let's try it. Tell him we're on our way."

"Hey, Eric, we're—"

"I heard him. Thanks. I'll let the front gate know. I'll be in the cottage with them. Just knock on the door when you get here. Thanks, Jack, I appreciate it, it'll mean a lot to her, to both of them."

"Back to the cottage," Dillon said.

Suel circled two blocks and headed back the way they'd come. They pulled into the parking area a short time later. Suel grabbed his briefcase from the trunk of the car, and they headed back toward the cottage. Berg-man answered the door just after they knocked, then stepped outside, closing the door behind them.

"Just a note of caution, the wife is really fragile. Please no detail on the event, no mention of the autopsy.

Just tell her things are progressing and when we have information, we'll relay it to the Senator. Okay?"

Suel nodded.

"Yeah, sure," Dillon said.

They followed Bergman back into the cottage, then down the dark-paneled hallway to the library. Just like before, Bergman knocked on the door, then stepped into the library as he said, "Detective Inspector Suel and US Marshal Dillon."

Fitzwilliam was leaning forward, talking softly to his wife. He turned and looked at them as they entered, squeezed his wife's hand, then stood and walked toward them. "Thank you for coming back on such short notice, gentlemen." He turned and looked at his wife. "Molly thought it best if she met you. We promise not to take up too much of your time," he said, sounding like he was maybe reminding Molly of a previous discussion.

She was a dark-haired woman who, under better circumstances, would have been referred to as attractive or pretty. Just now, she looked like she hadn't slept for a week. Her dark hair hung limply and was sort of off-center and standing up on top, still messed from her failed attempt at sleep. She had a haphazard part on the left side. Her eyes were puffy and bloodshot, with dark bags under them, and red-rimmed from crying. She wore a grey, two-piece outfit, a skirt, and matching jacket. The skirt and jacket were wrinkled, and there was a stain on the jacket that appeared to be from something spilled, maybe coffee by the looks of it. The outfit looked like she'd had it on for days. A cup of black coffee sat on the coffee table and appeared to be untouched. An oily sort of film coated the top.

"Molly, these are the men in charge of the investigation. They'll have to get back to work shortly to continue sorting through this, but they've taken a moment from their task to meet with you."

She bit her lower lip and nodded, then cleared her throat a couple of times. "Thank you for coming to see me, gentlemen. I'm sorry for the inconvenience. I promise I won't take up much of your time."

"It's not inconvenient," Suel said.

"Our deepest condolences," Dillon added.

"Brian, I wonder if I might have a moment or two alone with these gentlemen. I'd like to…."

"Molly, they really need to get back to work. Nothing is going to be accomplished while they're here with us."

She flashed a smile that was more along the lines of *"If looks could kill,"* then said, "Yes, as always, you're right. I'll make it as short as possible if you and Agent Bergman could give us just a moment. Please."

Dillon was going to say something, then thought better of it.

"We'll be just outside the door, dearest," the Senator said, then gave Bergman the nod, and they headed out the door.

She watched them leave, then once the door was closed, said, "Have a seat, gentlemen. Please forgive my appearance, but under the circumstances, I've been just a bit preoccupied. Where do things stand?"

They sat down on the couch, just opposite Molly Fitzwilliam. Suel looked at Dillon, nodded, and said, "Go ahead."

Thanks a lot, Dillon thought. "We're following a number of leads. We mentioned to your husband that we spoke on the phone yesterday to Josh Hughes and Jacob Schmidt. We spoke to them again today, asking for images of your son with his guitar and if they had any of just the guitar."

"Why?"

"One of the many angles we're following, and let me state that we are attempting to cover as much ground as possible, so one of the questions we have is, did someone take a fancy to the instrument? We're aware it's valuable, I think your husband mentioned a price tag of two grand. Might that have served as an incentive to someone? Maybe. We just don't know at this stage."

"Agent Bergman mentioned an image of the guitar to me. I don't have my computer with me, but if I can log on, I'll be able to access my iCloud and send that image to you, actually a number of images to you. Kevin was quite proud of his acquisition of the guitar. He worked so damn hard to get over here, didn't want to tell his father about it."

"So, you knew he was over here?"

She studied Dillon for a long moment, then visibly swallowed as if to steady herself before she spoke. "Yes,

I've known of his plan for the better part of a year. As a matter of fact, I encouraged him. He'd worked so damn hard to do this, he, he…." She was suddenly sobbing, and neither Dillon nor Suel knew what to do, so they did nothing and sat there for a very long minute.

"I'm sorry, please excuse me. Umm, is there, is there anything else I can do to help you? I'll send those images to you. I'm sure Agent Bergman will be able to access a computer for me. Anything else you need?"

Dillon handed her a business card, and Suel did the same along with Joe Carroll's from the Musicians' Union. "Our email addresses are on there. The sooner we get those images, the better," Dillon said.

"My deepest condolences," Suel said. "We won't rest until we find whoever is responsible, ma'am."

"Thank you. I'm putting all my faith in you, so please be sure you have the correct individual," she said. "Then, once you're sure, please go ahead and kill the bastard."

They rose off the couch, said, "Thank you for your time."

As they headed for the door, she called to them, "I've never been more serious with a request in my life, gentlemen."

Bergman and Brian Fitzwilliam were just on the other side of the door when they opened it. "Everything go all right?" Bergman asked.

"Yeah," said Dillon. "She's going to ask you to find a computer so she can send us some images of the instrument. Sooner we get that, the sooner we can start examining that particular link."

"Gentlemen, thank you. I'm sure we'll be in touch," Fitzwilliam said, shaking hands before he hurried back into the room to his wife.

"Let's touch base at the end of the day. Let me check into that computer. It shouldn't be a problem," Bergman said.

EIGHTEEN

Dillon's phone rang just as they drove back out through the security gates. He glanced at the number but didn't recognize it.

"Hello?"

"Oh hi, I'm calling about the email I just received from the Union."

"Yes," Dillon said, sitting up in the seat and nodding in Suel's direction.

"The guitar, what can you tell me about it?"

"Well, it belonged to "The Edge," and it's signed by him and Bono."

"So it's signed by both them, right?"

"That's my understanding. What can you tell us?" Dillon asked.

"Tell you? I'm not sure I understand. I'd like to make you an offer. I can give you fifteen hundred euros, cash, sight unseen for the guitar."

"Fifteen hundred euros? You're kidding."

"No, why? Have you set an asking price? I didn't see one in the email, and of course, I'd want to see a picture of the item, well, and examine it before I gave you the cash."

"It's not for sale," Dillon said.

"Not for sale? Did someone already snatch it up?"

"It's not for sale. We're trying to get any information we can on a band that— Look, did you even read the article? Someone was murdered."

"Yeah, I get it. Hey, tragic and all that, but doesn't it stand to reason that the individual who owned that instrument has no real need for the instrument anymore? I thought the least I could do was make a fair offer, you know, maybe help with expenses."

"How about this?" Dillon said. "No. Can't thank you enough for your time. Goodbye," he said and disconnected.

"What was that about?" Suel said.

"Jackass said he wanted to buy the guitar since the current owner no longer has a use for it."

"Bollocks."

They were halfway to Grafton Street when his phone signaled an email arriving. He glanced at the address, a series of letters and numbers that he didn't recognize. He opened the email anyway. There were five separate attachments, and a one-sentence note, *"Hope these are of some help. Guitar is a Fender Stratocaster."* The first image was of Kevin Fitzwilliam holding his guitar. He was all smiles and looked even younger than in previous photos.

"Email from Molly Fitzwilliam, photos of her son and the guitar," Dillon said as he clicked on the rest of the images, two of Kevin with the guitar, three of the guitar on its own.

It was an electric guitar, wood grain that at least in the images appeared to be almost orange with a black neck and a white pickguard. Two scribbles in blue ink were visible on the pickguard, presumably the signatures of Bono and The Edge.

"Well, it's unique-looking, I'll give you that," Dillon said. His phone rang a moment later. "Hello. Yeah, Joe, I did. They just came through. Yeah, one call, some idiot who wanted to buy the guitar because the current owner wouldn't have any further use for it. No, I'm serious. If you do, that would be great. Yeah, wonderful idea. Okay, I'll keep you posted," he said and hung up.

"Carroll got the images of the guitar and Kevin Fitzwilliam. He's going to put all of them in an email, label it 'Murder Update' and send it out. "We're bound to get some action, don't you think?"

"It can't hurt," Suel said, then slowed and turned onto Grafton Street. Grafton was one large pedestrian walkway with exclusive shops on either side. Suel drove up and over the curb, then down about twenty-five feet and stopped.

"You hop out, and I'll pull over. Fitzwilliam was playing just a few doors down, right across from the Disney store. Here," he said, handing Dillon the color photograph of Kevin Fitzwilliam. "You start checking with shopkeepers on this side. I'll take the far side."

Dillon hopped out of the car, waited while Suel pulled alongside the building, then walked back over. "I'll work my way down to the next cross street and meet you back here. I've a feeling this is going to go pretty fast," Dillon said.

"Yeah," Suel said, then crossed over and entered the first shop.

Dillon figured it might take thirty minutes to talk to the managers in the various shops. He was finished in closer to ten minutes and was on his way back to the car when he passed a group playing, two guitars, a keyboard, and drums. He watched them for a few minutes, showed Fitzwilliam's picture to some of the crowd, and came up empty-handed again.

When the group finished their number, they literally passed a hat around. Dillon approached one of the guitar players stacking their equipment on a two-wheeled dolly. The kid looked to be a similar age to Kevin Fitzwilliam, young.

"Nice job," Dillon said.

"Thanks. Always helps to have a nice crowd like this lot."

"You got a minute? I wonder if you've seen this guy around. Guitar player. His name is…"

"You a copper? You sound American."

"I'm a cop and American. This is the guy who was shot over on Dame Lane the other day. We're trying to get any information we can on him. Just wondering if

you may have seen him playing anywhere or with anyone.”

He stepped over and looked at the photo, studied it,
and shook his head.

“Any of this look familiar?” Dillon asked and took
out his cellphone. He displayed the images of Kevin with
the guitar and then the images of the guitar.

“Sweet bit of work on that guitar, man.”

“It’s signed by Bono and The Edge,” Dillon said.

“No shit? Hey, lads, c‘mer and check out your
man’s pictures.” The other three gathered around and
looked at the images on the cellphone. “Your man says
Bono and The Edge signed the guitar.”

“It’s yours, the guitar?” one of them asked.

“No, belonged to the guy shot over on Dame Lane
the other day. I’m working with the Guards. We’re trying to get in touch with anyone who may have seen him
or knows a band he did a session with. Apparently, they
paid him a hundred euros and wanted him to join them.
His name was Kevin Fitzwilliam.”

“Yeah, heard about that,” one of the guys said. “No,
can’t say I ever saw him. Like the guitar, though. I guess
it’d be a bit out of my price range.”

“Feck’s sake, you couldn’t afford the strings.”

“You play here regularly?” Dillon asked.

“We got a license if that’s your question,” the larg-
est of the group said. The sound of his answer expressed
an attitude.

"I didn't mean it like that." He held up the photo. "This guy played a couple of numbers right around here about four days ago, then someone either with the County Council or somewhere apparently told him to stop because he packed up his guitar and walked away. I'm guessing he didn't know you needed the license. That's why I'm down here, trying to find someone who might have seen him."

"Sorry, but we can't help. Was he playing on Dame Lane?"

"Not that we know of. We didn't find an instrument. CCTV footage had him walking alone. He wasn't carrying anything."

"Bit strange, that. Well, I wish you the best of luck. We've got to get to our next gig. We're down at the far end, lads."

"Let me give you my card. You think of anything or run into someone who might know, please have them give me a call," Dillon said and handed each of them a card.

The big guy with the attitude had a heavy-duty orange extension cord wrapped up and hanging from his shoulder. He took one of Dillon's cards and said, "Wish you luck in finding the knacker that did it. Come on, lads, we're late as it is."

Dillon watched as they headed off down Grafton Street toward the far end. Something didn't seem quite right, but he couldn't quite put his finger on it. He turned and headed up the street. He saw Suel from a distance, leaning against the side of the car, talking on his phone.

Suel disconnected just as Dillon reached him. "Any luck?"

"No," Dillon said. "Went through the shops in about ten minutes. No one saw him or remembered him. Talked to four guys playing down there, they didn't know a thing. There's something about them, but I can't quite seem to put my finger on it."

"You think they know something, and they're not talking?"

"No, nothing like that. I believe them when they said they'd never seen him. No, it was more what they were doing. You got those CCTV images of Fitzwilliam here?"

"Yeah, hang on a minute, I'll get them." Suel opened the trunk of the car, snapped open his briefcase and stepped back around with the manila file, and handed it to Dillon.

Dillon rifled through the stack of CCTV images until he came to the ones of Fitzwilliam playing the few songs on Grafton Street, just before he was stopped and packed up his guitar. "Check this out. Notice anything?" he said and handed one of the images back to Suel.

Suel studied the image for a long moment, shaking his head. "I'm not getting it. What's up?"

Dillon pulled out his cellphone, clicked on the email from Molly Fitzwilliam, and handed the phone to Suel. "Here, that's the guitar he saved up all the money for—

the one signed by Bono and The Edge. Damn thing is electric. That's not the guitar he was playing the other day on Grafton Street, that guitar is acoustic. Either he's got two guitars, or he borrowed one from someone."

"Or bought it or stole it," Suel said.

"The stealing would seem to be really out of character, and as for buying it, he's got a set amount of cash to make this a success. I don't see him putting a new guitar on his credit card."

"We can check that out soon enough," Suel said and pulled out his phone. "Bergman," he said a moment later and nodded at Dillon. "Suel here. Listen, can you check out what credit cards Fitzwilliam had? We know he had an American Express, maybe he had others as well. We're looking for the purchase of an acoustic guitar. Dillon noticed the images of him playing on Grafton Street are with an acoustic guitar, not the autographed one his mother sent us images of. If he didn't purchase the guitar, maybe he borrowed it from someone, possibly whatever band he had played with. You've got copies of the images of him playing in that stack of images we printed off, show them to his mother, see what she says, and let us know. We're wrapping up on Grafton Street. We drew a big zero."

Suel disconnected and put the file back in his briefcase. "I'm thinking we need to find that band he played with. Could be he borrowed the instrument from one of them."

As if on cue, Dillon's phone rang.

"Jack Dillon," he answered, and a moment later was nodding excitedly to Suel. "Yes, yes, that's right. Jinks?" he said, spelled it out, then said, "J-Y-N-X? Got it. Can we meet you? I'd like to— Where is that? Yeah, actually, we're not too far from there. Understood. We can be there in ten minutes. Thanks. Sean is it? No, please call me Jack, Sean. Thanks. Appreciate the call, we'll see you shortly," he said and disconnected.

"Please tell me it's positive," Suel said.

"Sounds like it. A guy playing over at Doheny & Nesbitts tonight. He starts playing at eight. He's there now. Says the band Fitzwilliam played with is called Jynx. He's got the drummer's name."

"We can be there in five minutes," Suel said. "Let me just pull out, and you can hop in." Suel climbed behind the wheel, then made a U-turn on Grafton Street with the flashing lights on. He slowly drove the short distance to the curb as pedestrians strolled around either side of the car. They got a couple of dirty looks from a hen party off to an early start, cautiously dropped over the curb and back onto the street, then took off.

NINETEEN

Doheny & Nesbitt's was a mere five minutes away on Lower Baggot Street. It was a three-story brick building with a large black awning over the front windows running the width of the building and advertising Guinness in bold white letters. A large, rectangular clock was attached to the front of the building on the second floor with the word "Doheny" across the top and "Nesbitt" across the bottom. Centered on the building on the second floor was a green sign with red neon letters that simply read "BAR."

Suel pulled partially onto the sidewalk across the street from the pub. "Maybe bring that file with the CCTV images," Dillon said, and they hurried inside.

The room was compact with people mostly standing, a lot of people standing. Opposite the bar, a shelf ran the length of the room. People were leaning against it and resting their pints on it. Dillon worked his way through the crowd to the bar, waved a bartender over and asked for Sean, then realized he had promptly forgotten the last name. "He's playing here tonight, a guitar player."

The bartender nodded, pointed to a dark-haired individual with his hair pulled back in a ponytail seated at the far end of the bar. He looked to be about fifty and appeared to be drinking a Coke. "That's him down there," the bartender said, then checked his watch. "He'll be playing in about ten minutes. Get you a pint?"

"Not at the moment, thanks," Dillon said and headed down the bar. Suel followed.

"Sean?" he said as he drew closer. The man looked up and blinked a couple of times, apparently coming out of whatever trance he'd been in. "I'm Jack Dillon. We spoke on the phone just a few minutes ago."

"You're American?"

"Yeah, but don't hold it against me. This is D.I. Suel," Dillon said, indicating Suel standing behind him.

"Listen, mind if we step outside? I can grab a cigarette before I start playing, and I'll be able to hear you better. You going for a pint?"

"No, better not, it's liable to be a long night. Get you one?"

He smiled and shook his head. "No. Much as I'd love one, it's been over twenty years, a love relationship that just wasn't very good for me," he said, then slid off his stool, grabbed his Coke, and headed for the door. Along the way, he got a nod from three or four people, telling one he'd be back to play in just a few minutes.

"Looks like you're quite popular," Dillon said once they stepped out onto the sidewalk.

Sean had set his Coke on one of the large wooden barrels in front of the building and was in the process of lighting a cigarette. He shook his head, pulled the cigarette from his mouth, and exhaled a blue cloud up toward the sky. "I'm a regular every week here, so I'm lucky enough to have some folks who haven't gotten tired of me, at least thus far."

"You said you knew the band that Kevin Fitzwilliam sat in with, Jynx, was it?"

"That his name, Kevin Fitzwilliam? Brennan didn't mention a name but said the kid was good, damn good. Had a guitar signed by Bono and The Edge, that's what got my attention, the guitar they mentioned in the email. Then they sent an update around with photos of the instrument. Looked to be a nice bit of work. Like I said on the phone, I didn't see the guitar or this American lad for that matter. But there can't be more than one lad with a guitar like that. And the email from the Union said he was shot the other day over on Dame Lane, by the Stag's Head?"

Dillon nodded.

"Bunch of knackers. Makes you wonder what in the hell this country is coming to. Shot the lad, in cold blood, in the middle of the damn day and no one knows a thing. Jesus Christ."

"Yeah, it's been a tough go so far." Dillon took out his phone, punched the screen a couple of times, and said, "Sean, let me add you to my contact list. Give me the correct spelling of your last name."

Sean gave him sort of a funny look and said, "Brown, B-R-O-W-N."

"No letter e on the end of it?" Dillon said with a straight face.

"No."

"And who is the guy you mentioned, the drummer with Jynx?"

"Name is Dolan, Robbie Dolan."

Dillon added the name to his contact list. "And his number?"

Sean gave him the number, then said, "Yeah, Robbie said your lad was quite the hit. They were playing not too far from here, place called Kennedy's. I guess he had the crowd in the palm of his hand, the owner or manager or whoever wanted him to come back. Offered him a gig, then Robbie and some of the others asked him to join up with them, said he'd think about it."

"Some of the others?" Suel said.

"What?" Sean said, took a long drag of his cigarette, then checked his watch.

"You said some of the others. That suggests that someone or some of the band weren't that excited about him joining up."

"Oh, yeah, but that was just Enda. He's always a negative bastard, a right pain in the arse. You want black he gives you white. You say yes he's automatically going to say no. Has a bit of the dark side to the artistic personality you might say."

"And this Enda, what's his last name?"

"It's Murray or maybe Murphy, now that I think about it, not really sure. Robbie will know. You talk to him, he'll set you straight."

"What does this Enda do in the band?"

"For Jynx? He plays lead guitar and sings."

"You think he might have viewed Kevin Fitzwilliam as competition? Might have been worried they'd kick him out and bring Kevin in?"

"I guess I never thought of it like that, but I suppose that could be a concern. Like I said, he's a right pain. You're not thinking he's the one who shot the lad, are you?"

"We don't know what to think at this stage, so we have to look at all angles."

"Jesus, well, he's just the sort of plonker who would do it. He can be miserable, that one, sure as hell. Bit of a temper on him as well." He took a long drag from his cigarette, then dropped it on the sidewalk and crushed it with the toe of his shoe. "I wish you well, lads. If you'll excuse me, they're a bit of a stickler for me starting on time."

"Sean, thank you for your help," Dillon said and extended his hand. Sean shook it, nodded at Suel, then hurried back inside the pub. A cheer rose up from the crowd as he entered.

"Popular guy," Suel said.

TWENTY

Dillon phoned Sean's friend Robbie Dolan while they were still out on the sidewalk in front of Doheny & Nesbitt's. He ended up leaving a message. He placed another call to him a half-hour after that, he and Suel were back in the office by then. He needn't have worried. He ended up leaving another message and then one more thirty minutes after that.

"Bastard can't be that busy. It's been over an hour and a half. He's gotta be ignoring my calls."

"Maybe he's like your man, Sean, and he's playing a gig tonight, in which case he may well have his phone turned off or on airplane mode or something. What do you think about what Sean said regarding this Enda character?"

"About him being a pain in the ass? I'm thinking it's not just the closest thing we've got to a motive, it's the only thing. I'm going to do a little research on him, see if anything comes up online. You going to hang here or head home?"

"It's only been fourteen or fifteen hours. Much as I find our office comforting and comfortable, I think I'm going to head home. See you tomorrow?"

"I wouldn't dream of missing it," Dillon said.

He Googled Enda Murphy and came up with dozens of profiles on everyone from a GAA goalkeeper, to a radio personality and an author. He spent the better part of an hour scanning through pages and pages of the same name but never came across a guitar player.

He found who he was looking for on the third page of Enda Murray listings.

The image was of an individual with a shaved head, a ginger-colored goatee, and two gold earrings in both ears. In the picture, he was playing a guitar on stage while smiling at a mob of young women apparently screaming their heads off in front of the stage. The description listed him as lead guitar player and vocalist in Jynx. It also listed a series of music awards he'd earned from 2001 to 2011, but none after that, which struck Dillon as somewhat strange.

Facebook had a Jynx page listing six members in the band including, Enda Murray as well as drummer Robbie Dolan. A cursory glance of the band photos seemed to suggest that Enda Murray was possibly the oldest member, and Dillon wondered if that meant he was also the leader of the band if indeed they even had one.

There was also a list of upcoming gigs. Tonight, Jynx was playing at a place called Sweeney's Bar, which interestingly enough was located on Dame Street, close to where Brian Fitzwilliam had been murdered on Dame Lane. Dillon printed off an image of the band showing

Robbie Dolan, the drummer, and Enda Murray, the gui-tar player with a temper. He checked his watch, figured he could stop for a pint on the way home and catch their act. He shut down his computer and headed out the door.

Sweeney's was located on Dame Street, 32 Dame Street, to be exact, barely one block from the Stag's Head and Dame Lane. They advertised themselves as a drinking pub with a music problem, and that turned out to be not too far from the truth.

The place was jammed, with live music on all three floors. Jynx was playing on the ground floor main stage, all six members of the band, Robbie Dolan on drums along with Enda Murray on lead guitar. As Dillon en-tered, Enda was in the middle of screaming into a micro-phone. Another guitar player, a bass player, a guy on keyboard, and a sax player rounded out the group. Along with the band, there apparently was a large contingent of fanatic groupies, all women, screaming at the foot of the stage and blowing kisses, apparently all directed at Enda Murray.

He'd single out one or two women and direct part of a verse toward them, which left them screaming. One woman lifted her top and bared herself, sans bra, to Enda's apparent delight. He licked his lips suggestively and smiled at her, then directed his attention to another woman on the opposite side of the crowd, passing on the good fortune as it were.

They played for close to an hour before they took a break. Dillon nursed the same pint of beer the entire time. They walked off-stage, and a moment later came out a side door and headed for the bar. Enda was suddenly surrounded by a half-dozen women waving bar napkins and, in one case, what looked like a thong, all asking for autographs. He ignored them all, and two security guys dressed in black coats, t-shirts, and trousers gently pushed the disappointed group back so Enda could pass.

He said something to one of the other guitar players. Dillon was too far away to hear what it was, but he thought he could read the word "bitches" on Enda's lips. He approached the bar and quickly put down two shots of what looked like whiskey, one right after the other, both in less than ten seconds, without so much as a blink.

Robbie Dolan had his hand around a pint of what looked like Guinness and seemed to keep a distance between himself and the other members of the band. Maybe a personality clash with someone, or all of them, or maybe he was just a loner. After five minutes everyone but Robbie Dolan made their way backstage. Dolan continued to nurse his pint and remained at the bar. If he was recognized by anyone in the crowd, they didn't seem to react, certainly nothing like the adoration Enda Murray experienced.

Dillon made his way through the crowd and over to Dolan. There was an open space at the bar on either side of him.

"Robbie Dolan?" Dillon asked as he stepped into the empty space next to him.

Dolan looked up and smiled, then said, "Hi, how you doing?"

"Just fine, thanks. Wanted to compliment you on your work up there. Very nice."

"Oh, thanks," Dolan said and looked halfway surprised. "You play?"

"Me, no, not at all, absolutely no talent, and you can count your lucky stars you've never had to listen to me sing. Actually, a friend of yours gave me your name."

"A friend of mine? Who?"

"He's playing over at Doheny and Nesbitt's tonight, Sean Brown."

"Oh, Sean. Yeah, we've known one another for years, play the odd job together. He's at Downey and Nesbitt's is he? I didn't know that."

"Yeah, actually, he gave me your phone number. I think I left three messages on your phone. My name is Jack Dillon."

"Look, Jack, no offense, but I'm in a committed relationship and I—"

Dillon half-laughed, "That's not why I called. I was hoping you could help me out with some information."

"Oh?"

"The name Kevin Fitzwilliam mean anything to you?"

"Oh Christ, the lad was murdered over on Dame Lane the other day. Tragic. Such a nice lad, and the talent, my God, but he put us all to shame. You're American?"

"Yeah, I am. I was wondering if you could tell me anything about Kevin? Where he was staying? How he met you guys? I believe you or someone in the band mentioned he had his guitar signed by Bono and—"

"Bono and The Edge. Yeah." He smiled. "He let us look at it, but wouldn't let anyone touch it. Beautiful instrument. He had a particular cloth, and he carefully wiped it off before taking it out of his case, then wiped it down again before he put it back in the case. He played a set with us, couple of sets actually. Oh, maybe a week back, pretty sure we were playing at O'Donoghues. God, they all run together after a bit."

"Was the band talking about making him an offer to play with you?"

"No offense, but what's with all the questions?"

"I'm working with the Guards. We're looking for whoever murdered Kevin Fitzwilliam. I'm just trying to learn as much as I can about who he was with, what he was doing up until his death."

"Hey, I don't know shit about any of that. I should really get back. We're on in just a minute, and there's hell to pay if you're late."

"I'm just trying to get some general information, Robbie. Maybe we could get together after your gig tonight, have a pint, just chat. If—"

"I really don't have anything else to say on the subject. I gotta go," he said and began to step away, leaving his almost full pint on the bar."

Dillon reached out and grabbed him at the elbow. "Here's the deal, Robbie. I'd really prefer to keep all of this quiet. Just a casual conversation between the two of us. Very private. If we can't do that, the next thing that's going to happen is that two Guards will come around and haul you into an interrogation room. That action is bound to become public, might cause even more friction between you and the rest of the band, and from what I could tell just watching, you sure as hell don't need that action."

"Oh, please don't, don't do that."

"Well then, let's talk. Tell you what, when do you finish up here?"

"Tonight? We're done at midnight."

"Perfect. Why don't we meet at The International for a pint? I'll buy. Say about twelve-thirty."

Dolan glanced over his shoulder, checking to see if any of the band guys were around. "This gets out and they'll kick me out for sure, and I'm already hanging on by my fingernails."

"I don't intend to tell anyone. See you at The International?"

Dolan let out a long sigh and said, "Okay. Just promise me you won't let any of the guys know."

"Scout's honor," Dillon said, then watched him as he hurried backstage. Five minutes later, they were back playing, going into a new set. Dillon watched for a few minutes then headed over to The International.

TWENTY-ONE

Dillon was seated in The International pub at a small round table with his back up against the wall. The file of CCTV images rested on the table next to his pint. The bar was maybe half full and had the hum of quiet conversation, no music or TVs. Two women sat at the table next to Dillon with a tourist map of Dublin City Center spread out in front of them. They seemed to be planning their next day, although he was unable to tell exactly because they were speaking Spanish or maybe Italian, he couldn't be sure which. He glanced at his watch. It was almost a quarter to one, and he was just about ready to give up on Robbie Dolan when the man stepped into the bar and scanned the room. Dillon gave a wave of his hand, and Dolan came over.

"Robbie, thanks for joining me."

"Not like you gave me much of an option," Dolan said, then glanced over at the women next to them with the map.

Dillon nodded at the bartender, who promptly grabbed a glass and began to pour a Guinness. "Robbie, I'm not accusing you, or for that matter anyone else, of anything. I'm just trying to get a handle on what Kevin Fitzwilliam was doing in Ireland. He——"

"He told us he came over to be discovered. Went on and on about Bono and U2, planned to replicate their activity. Not to confuse him with the facts, but I told him it took them about ten years and a lot of hard work to be discovered overnight. I think he had allowed himself a month, five weeks at the most."

"I think a month is correct, and I know that part of it. What I don't know is who he was working with, well, other than the night with you guys. I've got no idea where he was staying other than a bed and breakfast here in Dublin for his first forty-eight hours. So, how did he link up with you guys?"

"How? He ran into Conor at some pub. He plays session music at somewhere over in Dub 4 on Sundays and then does a solo there from eight till ten. They hit it off, he and Kevin, and, well, it was actually Conor who mentioned him to the rest of us and talked us into having him do a set with us a couple of days later."

"Conor is the other guitar player, blonde-haired guy with a big mustache?"

"Yeah, he——" The bartender came over with a pint of Guinness for Robbie, set it down in front of him and left. "Yeah, Conor talked him up to us. He was just going to play the one set, and that was going to be it. But he was so damn good. The crowd loved him, I mean they really did, went absolutely bonkers over him. By the end of the night, we were all talking it up to ask him to join us. He made no secret of telling us he was looking for a group. It looked like a dream come true for all of us."

"Even Enda?"

"Enda," he said, and took a number of swallows from his glass. "Here's the deal, Enda is the band. Hey, you saw the reaction from the crowd tonight. The women love him, much to Fiona's dismay. But they go crazy. Let's face it. It's because of the crowd we can bring in that we get the gigs like tonight. And we're all painfully aware that we get the crowd because of Enda. He's the star. Just in case we forget, he's there to remind us on an almost daily basis. So, when your lad played a set with us, mind you just a set, now, the place went wild, and Enda, the star, suddenly was not all that happy."

"So if everyone was talking up Kevin joining the band, did—"

"Enda didn't want to hear a word of it. Of course, the funny thing is he's been threatening to leave us for the last year. The plonker goes on some sort of rant on just about a weekly basis threatening to leave. Christ, it'd be the death knell for the rest of us, so when your man Kevin washed up on shore, we thought it was perfect timing. Enda could go on and pursue his solo career, and the rest of us thought we'd been delivered once we saw the crowd going crazy over your lad."

"Did Enda threaten him or anything?"

"Threaten? Oh, God, no. In fact, just the opposite, he had Kevin stay with him and Fiona at least for a couple of nights. Then we heard the news some plonker had shot him."

"Did you go to the Guards?"

"No, we didn't. At least I didn't. Enda said he talked to them. Left his name and phone number with them. I don't know if he heard anything."

"Tell me about this Fiona. Who is she?"

"Fiona," he scoffed. "Enda's latest. American, by the way. He's always got one hanging in the wings, another on center stage, and one heading off the stage. Fiona's on center stage at the moment. Hard to believe, based on the way Enda operates, but she's a bit of a control freak as well. Funny she wasn't at the gig tonight now that I think about it. Oh, well."

"Do you know how she reacted to Kevin?"

"Yeah, she didn't hide the fact she wanted to ride the lad. She's the one who talked Enda into inviting your lad in for a few days. Amazed she could pull it off, but one can only imagine what she did to convince Enda and accomplish the fact."

The lights suddenly flashed off and on in the pub. Dolan took a few more healthy sips and drained his glass. "That's the sign. I should be heading home anyway, early day tomorrow. You'll, ahh, keep this between the two of us, won't you?"

"I will, Robbie. I appreciate you making the time to talk with me, especially after the long day. Text me the names and numbers of the other band members, will you?"

"What do you want with them?"

"Same as with you, just want to talk to them. Kevin might have mentioned something to Enda or maybe Conor. I just want to cover all the bases. You've been a big help, and I promise we'll keep this just between the two of us."

Dolan seemed to think about that, then nodded. "Okay, I'll text that information to you. Thanks for the pint," he said and rose off the stool.

"Before you go, can you take a look at something for me?" Dillon said and opened the file sitting on the table. He quickly rifled through the pages until he came to the images of Kevin Fitzwilliam playing the guitar on Grafton Street. "This is Kevin the other day, on Grafton Street. Did he have this guitar with him when he played the set with you guys?"

Dolan glanced at the image and shook his head. "He played it for two numbers, but he didn't bring it. It belongs to Enda. I'm guessing he must have borrowed it from him. I know he liked it the night he sat in with us."

"And Enda lent it to him?"

"Looks like it. You'd have to ask Enda. We're all kind of funny when it comes to our instruments," he said, then seemed more than a little anxious to leave.

"Thanks for making the time, Robbie. I really enjoyed your performance tonight. You guys are great."

Dolan nodded, then left out the side door. Dillon lingered for a few minutes, reflecting on exactly what he had and had not learned before he headed out the same way.

TWENTY-TWO

illon was just pulling into the parking area in his front garden when his cellphone chimed. He pulled it out and looked at the screen. A text message from Robbie Dolan with the names and phone numbers of the other band members, along with the reminder to please keep it quiet. He sent a three-letter reply, "THX."

He unlocked the front door, and Lucifer immediately ran out. He took up a position next to the driver's door, looked at Dillon, then lifted his leg and went all over the door. Once that was accomplished, he squatted next to his puddle and left a deposit, then marched back into the house, refusing to even acknowledge Dillon.

Up in the bedroom, Dillon dropped his clothes on top of the growing pile of discarded items lying in the middle of the floor, collapsed into bed, and promptly fell asleep. At some point during the night, Lucifer settled onto the spare pillow next to Dillon's head and remained there until he woke to his alarm sounding early the following morning.

He was in the office just a little after seven that morning and was on his third cup of coffee when Suel came in the door.

"God, you look like absolute shite. You ever make it home last night," Suel asked, then set a white styrofoam tray on his desk.

"Thanks for those kind words, Paddy. Yeah, just long enough to put on a clean change of clothes, close my eyes for a minute or two, then hightail it back in here."

"Those are clean clothes?" Suel said.

"Supposedly. At least, the cleanest ones I have. Hey, I ended up at Sweeney's last night and—"

"You're kidding. God to be young and stupid. The day wasn't long enough already, so you decided to go for a pint? Any action?"

"Yeah, but not the kind you're thinking."

"Oh?"

"I checked out Jynx online last night, turns out they were playing a gig at Sweeney's. I ended up chatting with Robbie Dolan. He's the drummer in Jynx."

"The fellow you phoned a half-dozen different times? Don't tell me he actually called you back."

"Not really. The band took a break, and I cornered him at the bar, then chatted with him in The International once they finished the gig."

"So you hit it off, did you?"

"Let's just say it wasn't as contentious as it could have been. I did get some information along with names and numbers of the rest of the band."

"And?"

"And I plan to call them today and talk to all of them, in person. Dolan told me that Kevin Fitzwilliam was a big hit when he sat in for a set with Jynx. Their lead guitarist, a guy named Enda Murray, has been threatening to leave for the past year, and the rest of the band more or less thought Kevin would be their savior. He, Dolan, alluded to some potential jealousy with Enda Murray and at least suggested that Murray's current girlfriend appeared to have more than a passing interest in Fitzwilliam. He thinks she had Murray extend an invitation to stay with her and Murray, at least for a couple of nights. That guitar Fitzwilliam was playing in the CCTV images on Grafton Street, looks like he might have borrowed it from this Enda Murray."

"So it sounds like Enda Murray and his girlfriend were friends to Fitzwilliam."

"Maybe, maybe not. There's at least the potential for some jealousy with the woman's involvement, and this Enda didn't sound all that pleased when the audience reacted positively to Fitzwilliam. It sounded like he, this Enda, might be someone who's pretty high control and wants all the attention to be directed at himself, doesn't like to share the stage. I plan on talking to all of them today, leaving Enda Murray for last."

"You thinking he's our shooter?"

Dillon thought about that for a long moment. "I'm thinking there are some potential reasons he could be, but at this stage, that's just a guess. No facts to back it up. One of the many reasons I'd like to talk with the other band members first."

They chatted for a while longer, decided it might be better if Dillon talked to the band members alone. Not being an actual Guard, he might seem just that much less intimidating. Dillon sent the text message with the names and phone numbers to Suel's phone. Suel did a records search of everyone, but came up empty, not so much as a parking ticket on anyone in Jynx. He did an address search on everyone, and it turned out that Enda Murray lived just three blocks from Dame Lane, the closest of anyone in the band.

Was it possible that Fitzwilliam had been staying at Enda's the night before and left his wallet and cellphone there along with his prize guitar? It was close enough that maybe stepping out the door with a twenty in his pocket for a coffee and breakfast would be the natural thing to do.

"There is one more thing we should check on," Dillon said a couple of hours later. "Robbie Dolan said that Enda had contacted the Guards about Kevin having spent time at his flat. See if you can find any record of that. I did a perfunctory check in our records here and couldn't find a thing."

"He might have gone into a Garda Station and filed a report. That would be the normal thing to do, maybe even a day or so later. After the shooting, I think it was at least twenty-four hours before Fitzwilliam's name was even released to the public. Christ, if he filed a report, it's probably only now slowly making its way to us through the official snail's pace system."

TWENTY-THREE

Dillon placed a call to Conor Dwyer a little before eleven that morning. A sleepy voice growled, "Hello."

"Conor Dwyer, please."

There was a long exhale into the phone, then, "Whatever in the hell you're selling, I'm not interested."

"Conor, I'm not selling a thing. I'm calling to talk to you about Kevin Fitzwilliam. He was shot the other day on Dame Lane. He...."

"I know, he was killed, it was in the news. You sound American. You a reporter? You calling from the States?"

Dillon had the image of someone sitting up in bed, suddenly wide awake.

From somewhere nearby, a sleepy female voice said, "Who in the bloody hell is that?"

"Quiet, you."

"I'd like to chat with you, see if you might be able to fill in some blanks and...."

"Probably be wasting your time, I can't really tell you that much. I only knew your man for maybe a few days. Actually, I didn't really know him, just played a little with him. He sat in on a set with us one night. Really good, it's all a shame that…."

"Listen, Conor, I'm in Dublin working with the Guards. I'm going to need to sit down and talk with you. How 'bout we meet for breakfast, say forty-five minutes, you just tell me where and I'll meet you. I'm just trying to get some information put together, trying to learn what he was doing for the short time he was over here. There a place we can meet?"

"This morning?"

"Yeah. Sorry for the short notice, but I'm sure you can understand, I'm sort of pressed for time. You pick the spot, and I'll buy."

There was a pause, and then Dwyer said, "You know Brams Cafe? It's in Clontarf."

"Yes, I do," Dillon lied, then started to click keys on his computer. A moment later, the online site appeared. "St Aidan's Park Road, isn't it?"

"Yeah. I suppose we can meet there. Let me grab a shower, and I can meet you around noon. Will that do?"

"That'll do just fine. I'll see you there, at noon," Dillon said, but Dwyer had already disconnected.

TWENTY-FOUR

Brams Cafe was part of a two-story structure that ran the length of the block. The cafe storefront was third from the corner, with purple windows and door, a purple awning ran across the front, and the second floor was white stucco. Four purple tables, two on either side of the front door, rested under the awning.

It was a pleasant morning, and Dillon took a seat at one of the outside tables. He ordered a coffee, then pulled the image of Jynx out of his breast pocket and examined the face of Conor Dwyer for a long moment. He was halfway through his coffee when he spotted Dwyer coming around the corner.

He was blonde with hair that looked to be a uniform length all over his head, no more than an inch long. He had a Fu Manchu mustache that was brown rather than blonde, and Dillon wondered if his hair had been dyed blonde, then decided it was indeed dyed the closer Dwyer came. He wore the standard designer jeans, navy-blue, and manufactured to look worn, a long-sleeve button-down shirt that hung loose rather than tucked in. Dillon noticed the shirt didn't have a shirttail per se but instead was the same length all the way around. He wore some form of brown leather boot on his feet with a long narrow toe ridiculously upturned, at least in Dillon's opinion.

"Conor," Dillon called and gave a wave as Dwyer glanced through the glass partition on the sidewalk.

"Dillon?"

"Yeah," Dillon said, getting to his feet. "Thanks for making the time, especially on such short notice." He shook hands with Dwyer, then nodded toward the chair opposite him, and they both sat down. "Get you a tea to start?"

"That would be grand."

Almost instantly, a young woman in a purple apron that was an exact match to the storefront appeared. " Can I take your order? Oh, hi, Conor. "

"How are ya, Katie? Breakfast tea, and a full breakfast," Dwyer said.

"Same for me, but coffee instead of the tea," Dillon stared for a long moment as she left, then said, "Nice place. I just never get here as often as I like. You're a regular, it sounds like."

"At least once a week, Katie and I sort of know each other from before," Dwyer said but didn't elaborate.

"How'd you meet Kevin Fitzwilliam?"

"I play a gig Sunday nights at a pub called The Bridge. You know it?"

"Can't say that I do."

"It's a nice place. Owned by some rugby lads, so it's always jammed the day of a match. It's on Ballsbridge, down in Dub 4. There was a bit of session music before-hand. I got there early and sat in, and that's where I met Kevin. Funny, he was playing this fancy electric guitar without the amp, so almost no sound, you know. But I'm sitting next to him, and I'm thinking this lad knows his way around. We sort of chatted a bit, shared a pint after, and he ends up sitting in with me while I played my regular gig. Christ, I could barely keep up. People were calling their mates to get down there and hear him. Figured he was some big-name American rock star, like."

"I heard he was pretty good."

"'Pretty good' doesn't begin to cover it, not to mention just a right nice lad. Anyway, we get to talking over another pint, as you do, tells me he's over here trying to get discovered, like Bono and the boys. I'm gobsmacked at that point and tell him he should play with Jynx a couple nights later. So he does. That's about the size of it," Dwyer said, then sat back just as the waitress brought their food, two large platters that were almost deep dishes. They were white, rectangular things piled with fried eggs, toast, bacon rashers, black and white pudding, sausage and fried tomatoes. "Thanks, Katie. Could I have some milk for my tea?"

She nodded, set Dillon's plate down in front of him, and then his coffee. "Milk?"

"No, black is fine," Dillon said. "So, how'd the gig go with Kevin and Jynx?"

Dwyer took a forkful of sausage, stuffed it into his mouth and scoffed. "Mmm-mmm, sort of depends on who you talk to. The audience went mental. Just like at The Bridge, everyone was calling their mates to get down to the pub and hear the guy play. So, from that aspect, how'd it go? Beyond our wildest expectations. Not to bore you with band personalities, but one of our mates, frankly, is the reason we've had the success we've had. That said, he's probably the least happy of the six of us, and for some time he's been talking about leaving and going out on his own."

"Would that cause a problem?"

"Probably not for him, "Dwyer said and piled fried egg onto a piece of toast then stuffed almost the entire piece into his mouth.

"But for the band?"

"He's the big draw, we all know that, and we're fine with that. Fact is, we all make a decent bit because of it. But if and when he does ever leave, we're royally fecked. So, when we see Kevin getting the reaction he did, well, it's not rocket science to think he can be our new man, and Enda can go off and do the solo bit he's always telling us he wants to do."

"And was that going to happen?"

Dwyer thought for a long moment, loaded up another forkful, shrugged and stuffed fried tomato and black pudding into his mouth. He chewed for a moment, then swallowed and said, "That's the funny thing, suddenly Enda didn't want any part of it. Said he'd built the band to where it is today, and he wasn't leaving. This after a year of telling us he was planning on leaving. It was almost like we called his bluff."

"So that was the last you saw of Kevin?"

"That's even stranger because after basically voting down having Kevin join us, Enda tells him he can crash for a couple nights at his place while he goes out and looks for other gigs. You'd think he'd want nothing to do with your man, but he gave him a place to stay. I think he was still staying with them when he was shot."

"Them?" Dillon said.

"What?"

"You said *them*, Kevin was staying with *them*. Some of the other band guys live with this Enda guy?"

"Oh, God no. That wouldn't be good for anyone's mental health. No, Enda has a girlfriend. American, actually."

"Really."

"Yeah, thinks she's Irish, you know, like most Americans. Say's she's Irish, I mean anyway, her name is Fiona O'Sullivan. But she wouldn't know what or even who the Taoiseach is, let alone the President. Nice enough woman, easy to look at, but your man Enda is on the catch and release program when it comes to tarts."

"Oh?"

"Yeah, likes to play the field, and he does. I've known him for six, maybe seven years, never seen one last a year, most just a couple of months, and to his credit, there are an awful lot of them out there just waiting in line."

"He must be quite the guy?"

Dwyer shrugged. "Be hard to live with, but then what do I know?"

"Is he mean?"

"No, now I wouldn't say that. I don't think he'd beat them or anything if that's what you're suggesting. But he's got a hell of a temper, and he'd be more than happy to give you the silent treatment for a couple of days, maybe a week, then suddenly all's forgiven. We've all been there. In the end, it's always all about him. That said, the success we have is due largely to him, no question."

"Is he the leader of the band?"

"Mmm-mmm, not in so many ways. We all have an equal vote, supposedly. But like I said, our success is due to him. We all know that, and just in case, he never lets us forget it."

"This Fiona, how long has she been around?"

"Fiona? Not exactly sure. I know she was a student at Trinity, dropped out a month or two back. We, umm, all might have had a bit of a tumble or two with her, then all of a sudden she's moved in with Enda and they're an item. At least, she'd like to think so. But with Enda, who knows what he's thinking? Like I said, your man's always got a couple of them on the side."

"You know any other bands Kevin Fitzwilliam may have played with?"

"No, I don't. Not for lack of trying, he was doing some busker gigs on the street, but I don't think that worked out too well. Poor bastard, with that talent it was just a matter of time and folks would have been screaming to have him, then some plonker goes and shoots him. What the feck?"

"You going to stay with Jynx?"

"Me, yeah. We've had some rough spots, but sure now, what band doesn't? And we're still together. I think we're pretty solid. Like everyone, everywhere, we're just looking for that one big break."

"And you thought it might have been Kevin Fitzwilliam?"

"Humf, it could have been. Guess now we'll never know."

"You got any questions for me, Conor? I didn't mean to make it seem like you were getting the third degree."

"Not a bother. No, to tell you the truth, it's good to kind of go over all this, realize how lucky I am. Kevin, he was a nice lad. He sure as hell didn't deserve what happened to him. Probably some drugged-out bastard who wanted ten quid for his next buy, Jaysus. Would you mind maybe not mentioning this to the other lads? No need in anyone getting upset."

"You thinking, Enda?"

"I'm thinking the band doesn't need the hassle."

"I won't say anything if you won't," Dillon said. He extended his hand across the table and shook hands with Dwyer. "I wish you guys all the success in the world.

You're in a very tough business, and you seem to be doing pretty well."

"At least for the moment," Dwyer said and sort of laughed, although there didn't seem to be much humor in it. He nodded, stood, and then headed back the way he'd come.

Dillon watched him until he rounded the corner and disappeared. Katie, the waitress, suddenly appeared, placed the bill in front of Dillon, then gathered up the two platters. Dwyer's was clean, Dillon's was only partially eaten.

"Would you like a box for that?"

"No. Sorry, just not that hungry, I guess. You know Conor?"

"Only briefly. He's a musician, so you know how that goes," she said then left.

Dillon looked at the bill, twenty-five euros. He placed thirty on the table, set his coffee mug on top of the bills, and left.

TWENTY-FIVE

Over the course of the afternoon, Dillon met with three other members of the band, P.J. Kelly, Tommy Ryan, and Mick Doyle. The conversations ran pretty much the same as the ones he had with Robbie Dolan and Conor Dwyer.

Kevin Fitzwilliam had been a remarkable guitarist and singer who literally wowed the crowd the night he'd played with them. Enda Murray had let him move in for a few days while Fitzwilliam looked for gigs and hoped to be discovered. Fitzwilliam, based on Enda's vote, would not be offered an opportunity to join Jynx.

Dillon placed a call to Enda Murray and left a message. He left another message once he returned to the office late in the afternoon.

He was just coming out of the break room after placing the three tea mugs left on his desk in the break room sink when McCabe opened his office door, not looking too happy, and called out, "Suel, now." He glanced around the room as everyone kept their head down, and spotted Dillon coming out of the break room. He stared for a long moment, then motioned with his index finger and said, "You too."

Dillon and Suel took up the couch in McCabe's office. McCabe sat down behind his file-covered desk with a long sigh, swirled in his chair to face the two of them, and said, "So?"

Suel gave a long, loud exhale in reply and said, "It's moving rather slowly. Thus far, the witness interviews, 'witness' in this case being a very general term, have been less than informative. A number of people claim to have heard the shot fired, but amazingly no one saw anything. Not the shooter, not the body. First person actually on scene was one of the barmen at the Stag's Head who was rolling an empty barrel out to that stack on Dame Lane. He actually found the body and called An Garda Síochána. No telling how many people passed by, gave a laugh and probably thought the body was that of a drunk. Of those actually insisting they heard the shot fired, there were eight individuals. One couple flew back to Australia yesterday, that leaves six individuals. Of the six, we have a time-spread of nearly forty minutes and reports of anywhere from one to five shots fired. We've found no evidence, in any way, shape, or form, of more than one shot being fired. Dillon has been interviewing individuals who had a dealing with Fitzwilliam. I'll let him bring you up-to-date."

McCabe rotated his chair a few inches and leaned forward with his elbows on the desk. "Please tell me you have something concrete."

"Not really, sir. I've been interviewing members of a band called Jynx."

"Jynx?"

"Yes, sir. Six members. I've spoken to all but one. In a nutshell, one of them met up with Kevin Fitzwilliam. His name is Conor Dwyer. He, Dwyer, was playing a solo gig. The two of them seemed to hit it off. Based on that initial contact, Fitzwilliam is invited to play a set two nights later with the band Dwyer is in, Jynx. He's an instant success, has the crowd cheering, loving him. The band takes a vote on asking Fitzwilliam to join them, but one of the members, actually their star by the name of Enda Murray, votes against the action, so the offer to join is never made."

"Why did this Murray vote against it?"

"Not sure, exactly. They all admit Murray is the man who made the band. He's the big star. He's also been talking about leaving the band for at least the past year. Maybe he—"

"So, is he leaving?"

"Apparently not."

McCabe sat back in his chair, tapped his lips with an index finger, and looked off in the distance. "So he's been saying he's going to leave, then when an opportunity presents itself he doesn't act, is that right?"

"Up to a point, yes. What he does do, however, is offer Fitzwilliam a place to stay. Apparently, Fitzwilliam takes him up on it, and from what we know, that is most likely the flat he was staying in when he was shot on Dame Lane."

"Most likely? So you don't know for sure?"

"That's correct."

"And where, exactly, is this flat?"

"On William Street South, sir. Not far from the Trocadero."

"The Trocadero? That restaurant?"

"Yes, sir."

"But that's just a stone's throw from Dame Lane, not even. Have you searched the flat?"

"Not exactly, sir."

McCabe's face took on a reddish tint. "Not, not exactly? My phone has been shoved up my arse for the past two days, first by our people, then by the American Embassy, then the news outlets, bleeding RTE, the Irish Times, the Herald, the Irish Sun, the Irish Independent, the Garda Commissioner made a personal call, twice, and was not at all happy."

"Yes, sir."

"Why haven't you brought this individual in, questioned him? I'm presuming it's a him."

"It is, sir. I wanted to talk with him first, get a feel for him. I—"

"Get a feel for him? Bloody hell. How does this feel? My boot up your hairy backside. Get this individual, what the hell was his name?"

"Murray, sir. Enda Murray."

"Get that bastard in here, and let's find out what in the hell he's been up to."

"I've attempted to reach him, sir, but each time I call, I've been dumped into his message center. I've left two messages and—"

"Mother of Jesus," McCabe shouted. "Then for God's sake, go to his flat and haul him in here by the scruff of his neck. Is that too much to ask?"

"That was going to be my next move, sir. I was just hoping to…."

"For fuck's sake, and you call yourself a US Marshal. I want him in here within the hour, or I'm going to toss the both of you in a cell. Now you get your backside—" McCabe's phone suddenly rang. "Oh, Christ on a cross, go on, get out, get out."

Both Suel and Dillon hurried out of McCabe's office. As they left, Dillon heard McCabe say, "Yes, sir, just checking on that. I believe we're about to bring someone in shortly—"

"How do you think that went?" Suel asked.

"I've done better."

"Come on. I'll drive. We better have another car follow. Just in case we need—"

"I had hoped to start my meeting with Murray out on a little more positive note than hauling him into an interrogation room."

"I'd say the time for that passed about forty-eight hours ago."

TWENTY-SIX

It took a good forty-five minutes before they could get a team and a vehicle to follow them. They drove down to William Street South. Since it was a commercial area with plenty of pubs, restaurants, and absolutely no available parking, they ended up blocking the sidewalk with their vehicles.

"We'll make this fast. Hopefully, he'll come along quietly. We'll get this all sorted and move on," Suel said. They were huddled around a blue painted door set between a pub and a Thai restaurant. Four buttons on the wall next to the door were labeled 'A,' 'B,' 'C,' and 'D' for the four apartments on the second floor. "Which unit is he in?"

"I've no idea," Dillon said. "The file just had the street address, not the apartment number."

"No…Bloody system, for feck's sake," Suel said, then punched the button for unit A and held it down for a long moment.

"Yes," a woman's voice said as soon as he removed his finger from the button.

Suel seemed to think for a brief second, then said, "Delivery, ma'am. For unit A."

"A delivery? I'm not expecting anything."

"This is thirty-four William Street South, unit A?"

"Who is it addressed to?"

Suel raised his hands up, made a face, then said, "Afraid the label's been torn. Lucky I've even the address here."

"Well, that's my address, but I— Tell you what, go ahead and leave it at the door and I'll—"

"I'm afraid I'll need a signature, ma'am. I can tell you the package looks a bit fancy if you ask me. From some fellow named Louis Vuitton. Maybe you know him."

One of the uniformed Garda quietly laughed and shook his head.

"Louis Vuitton? Hmm-mmm, I'll be right down."

"Well done," the officer who'd laughed said.

"Here, you better stand by the door. She sees the uniform, she's more likely to open the door," Suel said.

A moment later, a blonde woman, in a blue sort of silk dressing gown with her hair in rollers, cautiously came down the stairs. She wore fuzzy blue slippers on her feet. She grew a questioning look on her face as she approached the door, seemed to think for a moment, then, seeing the uniformed officer, opened the door. She looked to be about mid-thirties, and even with the rollers in her hair appeared very attractive. She drew the silk dressing gown tighter, crossed her arms over her chest, and did not look happy. "Is this your idea of a fecking joke?"

"No, ma'am," the uniform said, took a step backward and looked at Suel for a lifeline.

"Sorry to bother. We may have the wrong unit. Enda Murray?"

"That musician plonker? He's in unit C. This is about the noise, isn't it? We've all complained. Bollocks plays that damn guitar morning, noon and night, been at it for hours right now. I didn't think the landlord was going to do anything about it. It's been over a fecking year since we started to complain. Well, come on in, better late than never," she said, then stepped aside and held the door open.

The uniforms nodded and hurried up the stairs. Suel followed and said, "Thank you."

Dillon brought up the rear, said, "Thank you. Sorry to disturb."

"Mmm-mmm, what's your name?"

"Dillon, Jack Dillon."

"Not hard on the eyes," she said as Dillon started up the stairs.

The uniforms and Suel took a right at the top of the stairs and quietly moved down the hall in the direction of the guitar music. Dillon took just a step in the same direction, then turned as the woman came to the top of the stairs.

"I didn't catch your name," Dillon said.

"Claire," she said. "My friends call me Claire."

"Dillon," Suel called in a harsh whisper.

"Nice to meet you, Claire. We'll get this noise situation dealt with."

"Much appreciated," she said, smiled, then turned and walked in the opposite direction to the far end of the hall. As she walked, she placed one foot directly in front of the other, like a fashion model walking down a runway. Dillon appraised the view for a moment.

"Dillon, you wanker," Suel called in another harsh whisper.

They were gathered around the door to unit C. Suel shook his head as Dillon approached. "Might serve better if we paid attention to the purpose of our visit."

"I was thinking we may just need cooperation from the other residents, and made an effort to get on her good side."

"Yeah, that's what you were curious about, her good side. All right, everyone ready?"

They all nodded. Suel knocked, then stepped to the side so the uniforms were showing should someone look through the keyhole. The guitar cords kept playing for maybe another twenty seconds. Just long enough to suggest the player didn't plan to answer until he was finished with his piece.

Suel was just about to knock again when the music stopped. A moment later, the door opened, and there stood Enda Murray in all his glory. Shaved head, two gold earrings in each ear, ginger-colored goatee, shirtless, barefoot, and wearing red silk boxer shorts. The boxers had a series of concentric black circles forming a target, with the bulls-eye dead center over the fly opening.

"Mister Enda Murray?" Suel asked.

"Who wants to know?"

"An Garda Síochána, Mister Murray, we'd like you to come with us. We've a few questions about—"

"I haven't done shite, and you damn well know it. That bitch is lying her ass off."

"If you'd come with us, please, I'm sure we can sort this all out."

"Apparently, you weren't listening. I haven't done anything."

"Sir, one of our officers will accompany you while you get dressed, then if you'd be so kind as to come with us, we can get this over with and bring you back to—"

"I can't go with you bastards if you bothered to check the website you'd know I've got a gig tonight."

"I'm sorry about that, sir. If you'd hurry and get dressed, there's a good chance we can have you back in time for your gig."

"Come on, damn it. She put you up to this, didn't she? Whatever she said, the bitch is lying. I haven't done a thing, and I never touched her."

"Sir," Suel said and smiled. The smile conveyed anything but warmth and friendship. "Now, I'm not going to ask again. You can get dressed, or you can get hauled out here and down onto the street dressed like that." Suel nodded at the red silk boxers. "Your choice."

Murray seemed to consider his options, then said, "Wait here," and began to close the door. Suel blocked the door with his foot, then shouldered the door open. It bounced off the wall with a loud bang.

"What the—"

"Go with him while he gets dressed," Suel said to the Guards. "Two minutes, Murray," Suel called as both Guards followed him down the hall. He seemed to pick up his pace slightly at the sound of Suel's voice. Suel looked at Dillon and whispered, "Absolute asshole."

A high-pitched scream suddenly came from down the hall. Dillon and Suel looked at one another, then began to head down the hall only to be met by a naked red-headed woman running toward them.

"You bastards," she said, holding a too small pillow in front of her. "What are ye doing?"

"Fiona O'Sullivan?" Dillon said as Suel produced his ID and badge.

"Who? No, Margaret Kenny. Oh God, can you get me my clothes? They're back in the bedroom. Look, I just maybe had a little too much to drink earlier, and umm, I shouldn't be here." She whispered that last part and then looked frantically down the hall.

Dillon looked at Suel, who nodded, and he headed down the hall to the bedroom. Murray was in the process of pulling a t-shirt over his head. Dillon picked up a pair of white jeans and a silky red top from off the floor. A pair of red heels were partially under the bed next to a pair of handcuffs. Murray was sitting on the end of the bed with his back toward Dillon. Dillon raised his eyebrows at the cuffs, and the two Guards smiled. He gathered up the shoes, looked for any undergarments for a second or two, then went back to Suel and naked Margaret Kenny.

She dropped the pillow, grabbed her clothes from Dillon, then rifled through them, looking for undergarments. She frowned then quickly pulled the top over her head. She struggled into the tight white jeans, moving her hips from side to side as she slowly slinked them up her thighs, then slipped into the red heels. She picked a purse off the floor next to the door and said, "May I go now?" sounding more like she was making a demand than asking permission.

"Absolutely, Miss Kenny. Thank you for your co-operation." Suel smiled.

She hurried out the door and down the hallway.

TWENTY-SEVEN

Murray reappeared with a Guard on either side of him a moment later. This time he was dressed in blue jeans and a white t-shirt that had greyed and looked like it hadn't been washed since the first of the year. He wore a pair of orange Nikes on his feet. "There, happy? I'm dressed, and you chased off the afternoon's entertainment."

"Much better. We appreciate your cooperation. Let's be off," Suel said and headed back down the hall. One of the Guards followed. The other Guard gave Murray a gentle shove to get him moving.

"Watch it. No need for the rough stuff, bollocks," Murray said, then headed down the hall with the Guard behind him shaking his head. Dillon closed the apartment door behind the three of them and brought up the rear.

Down on the sidewalk, the Guards opened the rear door of their vehicle for Murray. "Oh, isn't that just sweet. Who knew you had any manners?" he said as he climbed into the back seat.

"Mr. Murray, if you'd find the ride more comfortable with a pair of handcuffs, I'm sure we'd be more than happy to accommodate."

"Piss off," Murray said and made a face like he smelled a fart in church, but he didn't say anything else.

Suel stared at him for a long moment, then closed the rear door. "Take the bastard into interview room three. Take your time getting there, and processing him in. He's not under arrest at this point. No phone calls until after we arrive. Let the big prick stew for a while."

They stood on the sidewalk and watched the Guards as they backed up. Murray glared out the window at Suel, who brought his right hand up to about shoulder height and wiggled his fingers in a ridiculous sort of wave.

"Why are you antagonizing him?" Dillon asked.

"Because I don't like the bastard. He's impressed with himself, and for the life of me, I can't figure out why. Plus, he had a gorgeous naked redhead in the bedroom, and the plonker is sitting around in his underwear playing a guitar. When was the last time you had a naked redhead waiting in bed, and you thought it would be a better idea to play a guitar?"

"Well, never, I guess, it's just that—"

"It's just that he thinks he's one of those privileged little pricks who's better than the rest of us. I'm sure he's never made a mistake, just ask the bastard."

* * *

Suel and Dillon had been waiting at the processing desk for twenty minutes. It was maybe a ten-minute drive from Murray's apartment. When he finally did arrive, he was crimson-faced, and a Guard had hold of either arm.

"You two," Murray shouted. "I want my solicitor, right fucking now."

"Soon as you're processed, Mr. Murray. For your own protection, it's how we do things. Looking out for your best interest. I'm sure you understand."

"Why am I under arrest? What the hell did I do?"

"You're not under arrest, Mr. Murray, we just want to talk with you. Now, as soon as we record your presence, we'll get you in an interview room, and we can get started. The sooner we get started, the sooner we can get you home. But I'm afraid none of that can happen without cooperation, Mr. Murray, cooperation."

"For Christ's sake, we were driving around up in Finglas. You think I don't know what you're doing here? I already told you, whatever the bitch said is a lie. Now I'm not going to say another word until I talk to my solicitor."

"Then it's liable to be a very long night, Mr. Murray. We'll see you in interview room three," Suel said, then turned and walked down the hall.

"Hey, hey. Get back here. I'm not through with you yet. Hey, did you hear me? Get back, hey—"

TWENTY-EIGHT

Interview room three was a dim, damp room with the dank scent of sweat and fear permeating the grey painted walls. A fluorescent light fixture blinked intermittently and, if one listened carefully, gave off a quiet but constant buzz. One wall was dark tinted glass, behind which was a viewing room. A grey metal tray on wheels with three shelves holding recording equipment was sitting over in the corner. A large, grey, metal-topped table was placed in the center of the room with four chairs, two on either side. The chairs on the side facing the door were bolted to the floor, and Murray sat in one of them, looking less than happy.

Suel and Dillon sat quietly in the two chairs opposite him. They'd been enjoying one another's company in the interview room for fifteen or twenty minutes. Every once in a while, Murray would sigh and half-whisper something like, "Christ."

Dillon and Suel didn't react.

Finally, Murray said, "I told you, I'm not going to say shite to you until my solicitor is here," breaking the silence.

Suel gave a long sigh and said, "And I told you, Mr. Murray, we just want to chat. You're not under arrest at this point, but we can, and will, hold you for forty-eight hours if you…."

"This is absolute bullshit. Do you know that? Whatever the bitch told you, I didn't lay a hand on her. You know how they are. At first, they say it's all about sex, and then one morning you wake up, and they want to know what your intentions are. Christ, if it wasn't for the sex, I'd swear—"

"Then I'm afraid it's going to be a rather long night," Suel said, and sat back. He tapped Dillon on the ankle with his foot.

Dillon had been sitting quietly for all of the fifteen minutes. "Mr. Murray, would you like a cuppa?"

"What?"

"I said, would you like a tea? You don't have to talk, Christ, you can just nod your head if you want some, but I could go for a tea, maybe a biscuit or two. Paddy," he said, turning to Suel. "Would you do the honors?"

Suel frowned, but got to his feet and started for the door.

"I'll take mine with a little milk," Dillon said. "You?"

Murray paused for a moment, looked at Dillon, and then said, "Milk, but not too much."

"And some biscuits for the both of us," Dillon added, then raised his eyebrows to Murray.

Once Suel left the room, Murray seemed to relax. He slouched just a bit, cranked his neck from left to right. He stared at Dillon for a long moment, then said, "Is this supposed to be the part where you show me you're the good cop, get me to talk?"

"Not really. It's more like this is the part where I get some tea and biscuits because we've been working all day, and I'm starving my ass off. By the way, no offense, but that redhead, Margaret Kenny, sorry we interrupted, she was a looker."

Murray halfway smiled, "Was that her name? Margaret Kenny?" He repeated her name, sounding like he was memorizing it. "Yeah, she would have been fun. I had this tune bouncing around in my head, and when that happens, I just have to get it out—"

"The tune?" Dillon said and smiled.

Murray smiled back and said, "Yeah, I was talking the tune. So you're an American?"

"Yeah?"

"Bitch must have told one hell of a story to have the likes of you brought over."

"What?"

"Come on, how stupid do you think I am? Fiona, she…."

"I don't know any Fiona."

"You don't know Fiona O'Sullivan?"

"No."

"Then why the hell are you even here? Why am I here?"

"Kevin Fitzwilliam."

"Fitz— I didn't have anything to do with that. Are you crazy? I—"

"I know that. We know that. We're just trying to get information, put together his last few days is all. So far, the little we know is that you were kind enough to let him crash at your place for a night or two. Sounds like you were helping him out. We're just trying to find out if he ended up somewhere else or with someone. But when you did that routine on Suel back at your flat, well, he started thinking there might be more to this."

"Fitz crashed with us, with me, for two nights. He never made it back the third night. I guess that was 'cause he'd been shot. But I didn't find out until later that he was the one who'd been shot, been killed. I went to the Garda station over on O'Connell Street a day or two later, gave them my name and address. I didn't know he'd been shot at the time. His guitar was still at my place, it's still there, and I just filed a report. I was afraid Fiona would say I stole the thing."

"God, I know how that can go," Dillon said, trying to sound sympathetic. "Had she been with you long?"

"A few months. It was getting to be time for her to move on, anyway. She was over here on a student visa. Of course, she dropped out about three weeks into her studies. The visa was just about to run out, and she was pushing to get married so she could stay in Ireland."

"Married?"

"Yeah, ain't that just about the dumbest thing you can think of? Don't get me wrong, she was fun, good in the sack, great in fact, but I'm not the marrying type. Playing our gigs, I can have a different piece every night if I wanted. Too bad I've to earn a living, it would be a great life," he laughed.

"So her visa expired, and she went home?"

"Not exactly," he laughed. "She told me she rode your man Fitzwilliam just to get back at me for not wanting to marry her. I figured fine. You're riding him, then get your arse out the door. Not that I cared, really. I just don't like being told what to do, you know? So she ups and leaves, storms out of the place, says she'll get even, calling me all sorts of shit. She had a couple of weeks left on the visa. I got no idea where she went. She's probably either sleeping with some other wanker or already back in the States. Who knows?"

"They can be a lot of work," Dillon said.

"You're preaching to the choir on that one. Course, once I heard Fitzwilliam had been shot, and all I'm thinking is, Jaysus, I'm glad she's gone. Talk about divine intervention."

"She's a temper?"

"You kidding? You've no idea what she's like. The bitch would throw things, scream bloody murder, then turn round and ride you till you thought you wouldn't make it through. She'd tell me about the guns her family had, the old man and her brothers. Damn Wild West.

God, I'm thinking they're all nuts and, well, she never proved me wrong."

"There's a lot of that over there."

"I didn't believe her at first. Told me she learned to shoot when she was just seven or eight. Christ, I've never held a gun in my life. In fact, I told her that, so what's she do? She wants to take me out shooting."

Dillon put a surprised look on his face.

"Yeah, I know. Like shooting up the place is going to be a fun time or something. I mean, are you fucking kidding me?"

"Shooting?"

"Yeah, we're out in the country, on my cousin's farm, big family party a couple of weeks before his wedding. Says she wants to do me in a field, I guess she saw that in a movie or something. So I figure, yeah, bring it on, baby. We're out walking. She's got a bottle of wine in her backpack. We finish the wine. She sets the empty bottle up on the stone wall just pretty as you please. She takes her top off, and I'm thinking here we go. Then she steps back about ten feet and pulls this little pink gun out of her backpack. Thing's so small it looked like a toy."

"A little pink gun?" Dillon said and felt his heart suddenly racing.

"Just a tinchy little thing, and it's pink as a baby's bum. She could damn near hide it in her hand, and she isn't a big woman."

"Pink?"

"Yeah, and it shot silver bullets. God, you Americans, you're all fecking nuts."

"I show you a picture of this gun, could you identify it?"

The door suddenly opened, and Suel stepped back in. "Tea and biscuits for the loving couple."

Murray seemed to stiffen up and grew quiet.

TWENTY-NINE

Dillon turned and smiled at Suel as he walked toward them. He carried a steaming tea mug in each hand and had a box of chocolate-covered biscuits tucked under his arm. Dillon's back was to Murray, and he kept signaling the door to the room with his eyes, hoping Suel would pick up on it.

"There we go," Suel said, setting both mugs down on the table. He slid one halfway across toward Murray, set the box of biscuits down in front of Dillon, and said, "Be back in a bit, the boss wants to see me. Christ almighty." Then he gave a wink and hurried out of the room.

"Humf," Murray said as Suel closed the door behind him. "Hopefully, your boss will ream the bastard a new one."

Dillon slid the box of biscuits a bit closer to himself, then took a sip of tea and grimaced. "Oh, God." He opened the box of biscuits, held it toward Murray, who took three.

Murray looked around the room and chuckled. "Yeah, I'm guessing they're not known for their tea around here. Funny seeing your reaction, Fiona was the same way, didn't like the shite. She'd fill half her mug with sugar then force it down, pretending to be Irish. Piece of work, that one," he said, then took a long slurp from his mug.

"So you weren't kidding? Your woman actually has a pink gun?" Dillon said, trying to get the conversation back on track.

Murray nodded, swallowed. "Like I said, you Americans, you're all crazy. You can't make this shit up."

"And the bottle, did she ever hit the thing?"

"The wine bottle? Oh yeah, shot five or six times, never missed. Hell, I'm still not sure if she was showing off or sending me a warning. Funny, each time she shot, the bottle got smaller, but it never exploded, you know, like it does in the movies. Couldn't have taken her more than five seconds to get a bunch of shots off, shooting just as fast as you please, never missed once, and when she finished, there was just a pile of glass left on the wall."

"How was your shooting?"

"Me? I told you, I've never held a gun, and I wasn't about to start then. Besides, the shooting got her all turned on and hot. We were going at it about a minute later. I thought that was a little more fun than blowing up some fecking empty wine bottle. She tried to give me some shit about it later on, but I told her the ride she gave me was a lot better than shooting some gun. She liked that comment," he said and reached for the box of biscuits.

"Where'd she get the thing?"

"The gun?" He stuffed another biscuit into his mouth and shrugged. "You got me. I guess she brought it in from the States. I think she said she flew into Paris from the US, probably had it in her luggage. Took a boat over from France to here. It wouldn't be that hard. She told me all sorts of shite about the thing, but it went in one ear and out the other. I mean, she's pulling her jeans off and talking about this pink girlie gun. Guess what I'm going to be paying attention to? They're all nuts, but thank Good never quite cop on to the power they have."

Dillon nodded.

"Enda, Kevin Fitzwilliam was shot between half-past twelve and one in the afternoon. Here's the deal, you said Fiona had sex with him and told you it was because you wouldn't marry her, then you kicked her out of your flat."

"Yeah, who wouldn't? I mean, what a bitch, riding everyone who gave her a second look," he said, shook his head and reached for another biscuit.

"Some folks are gonna think you might have been the guy who shot Fitzwilliam. You know, 'cause you were pissed off about him and Fiona hopping in the sack. What can I tell 'em, so you don't get in trouble?"

"Shoot the guy? Fitzwilliam? Feck's sake, I don't have a gun. You been listening at all? I just got done telling you I never, ever, shot one, never so much as held one."

"But you had access to Fiona's gun. You see what I'm saying?"

"But I threw her out by then. She was gone. Besides, I was busy when your man was shot."

"Busy?"

"Yeah, my culchie cousin, I played at his wedding that day."

"With Jynx?"

"Jynx? Are you mad? No, the wedding was in the damn church, down in Wexford. I took the bus there, played at the service, then got a right piss on that night. Ended up with this blonde one who had a great big tattoo right on her—"

"People saw you at the wedding?"

"Saw me? I was playing guitar up on the altar. Your priest was younger than me, clapping his hands, getting everyone dancing in the aisle. I told him he was in the wrong business, should be doing gigs with us up here in Dublin."

"So folks can attest to the fact you were there."

"Yeah, you listening? I just told you. Ninety, maybe a hundred people at the wedding. I was the music, I made the event memorable, made the whole thing rock, play-ing all my original stuff. Couldn't get enough pictures of me. Someone posted a video of me in the church. It's up on YouTube. Course the bastards forgot to mention my name and won't answer my emails now."

Dillon turned in his chair and motioned at the wall with the tinted windows. A moment later, Suel came bounding into the room.

THIRTY

Dillon and Suel had Murray go through the entire tale again, three separate times. They both took notes, taped the conversations, and tried not to interrupt too often. When Murray had finished the third time, Suel said to Dillon, "Be nice if we had some proof that would link that handgun to the shooting." He turned to Murray and said, "We can prove you were at the wedding. That's your alibi, gets you off the hook."

"So there's your proof right there. I'm free to go, right?"

Dillon said, "You think the glass from the bottle could still be sitting on that wall?"

"Don't know why it wouldn't be. The field is out in the back of beyond. After all, it's not like she wanted people to watch me riding her. The girl's got a bit of the kink in her, but having mates watch has never been a hot button with her, least as far as I know."

"The spent casings might still be there," Dillon said to Suel. "We get those, get a match to the casing we found on Dame Lane, we're halfway home."

"Casing?" Murray said.

"The shells she fired, I'm guessing she didn't pick them up."

"Yeah, the silver bullets. I told you they'd already been shot. They're worthless," Murray said and shrugged.

"We need to get someone down there," Dillon said.

"More importantly, we need to put a stop to her trying to leave the country. That's if she hasn't already gone," Suel said.

"She'd fifteen or twenty days left on her student visa when I gave her the boot, and she sounded pretty straight on not overstaying. I think they put the fear of God in them at the school orientation."

"Was that at Trinity?"

"Yeah, but like I told you, she was out of there in two or three weeks. Little more interested in partying with a star than cooling her heels in a classroom," Murray said, smiled, and sat up just a little straighter.

"You know where she lived at Trinity?"

"No," Murray said, shaking his head. "She only mentioned it in passing, maybe just once or twice."

Suel pulled out his cellphone and punched in a bunch of numbers, then checked his watch. At this point, it was close to ten. They could hear the phone ringing on the other end of the line. A moment later, a recording came on, dumping Suel into a message center.

"Mary Pat, this is Paddy Suel. Working a case, and I need your help. Please call me as soon as you get this, no matter the time," he said, then left his phone number.

He sent a text message with the same information, then looked at Dillon and Murray.

"I'm not going to hear from her until tomorrow morning. She's on staff at Trinity. I'm thinking we can find out where this Fiona was staying before she moved in with you. In the meantime, Dillon, you contact Bergman. See if he can't get an alert to hold this Fiona if she hasn't already left the country or, worst scenario if she's already in France. We get that done, maybe you could take an early morning drive down to Wexford, see if you can recover the bits of that wine bottle and the spent casings."

"If you want, I could go with you, show you where she shot the shit out of that bottle."

"Really?"

"You kidding? Me solving the murder of a fellow musician, you got any idea what this can do for my career? I couldn't buy that kind of press."

Suel looked skeptical.

"Oh, come on. I mean, I pretty much gave you the woman on a silver platter. The least you can do is let me tie up a couple of loose ends for you. I love a good mystery. I've watched all the episodes of Farr, for Christ's sake."

"Farr?" Dillon said.

"An RTE crime show set in Belfast. Don't even ask," Suel said.

"Come on, I can save you time. I told you this place was out in the back of beyond. You'll never be able to find it without me."

"How long does it take to get there?"

"A good two hours if you know where you're go-ing," Murray said. "And you don't."

"Yeah, okay, you can come along, but I'm picking you up at five."

"In the morning?"

"Yeah."

"For feck's sake, many's the night I'm not even home by that hour."

"Lucky you." Dillon turned toward Suel and said, "How 'bout I give Mr. Murray here a lift home. You can tidy up the recording."

"Recording?" Murray said.

"Wanted to make sure we didn't go and violate your rights," Suel said with a wicked smile.

Murray looked like he didn't believe him, but had no idea how to answer.

"Come on, I'll give you a lift home. I'll be picking you up tomorrow morning at five on the dot."

Dillon parked on the sidewalk in front of the blue door leading up to Murray's flat and got out of the car.

"Thanks, but I think I can make it from here," Mur-ray laughed.

"Just want to make sure. I'll escort you upstairs."

"Hmmm-mmm, police protection, just like all the big stars. I could get used to this."

"Get going," Dillon said, then followed Murray up the stairs and down the hall to his apartment.

"I'll see you in the morning," Murray said as he opened his door. "Say, just a thought, you mind if I take some pictures tomorrow?"

"Pictures?" Dillon said.

"Never mind. Me taking pictures, dumb idea, forget it."

"See you in the morning. Be ready. I don't want to waste any time, and I'll need to get back up here to Dublin as fast as possible."

"We'll be ready," Murray said, then stepped inside and closed the door.

Dillon waited a long moment, didn't hear anything out of the ordinary, then went back down the hall to unit A. He thought about his next move for a moment then knocked softly on the door. He stood there for maybe a minute but didn't hear anything from inside. He slipped a business card between the doorframe and the doorknob and headed downstairs.

Back in the car, he pulled out his cellphone and called Bergman.

"Dillon?" was how he answered the phone, then he cleared his throat, suggesting he'd maybe been asleep.

"Eric, hi. Sorry about the late hour. I think we got something."

"God, promise? I don't know about you, but I'm feeling pressure and a lot of it."

Dillon went on to explain their interview with Murray and the news about Fiona O'Sullivan and her pink handgun. "I'm driving down to Wexford with Murray early tomorrow morning. I want to get there at daylight, and hopefully, I can recover those spent casings and the remnants of that wine bottle. Compare the casings to the one we recovered on Dame Lane."

"Where is she now?"

"That's the other reason I'm calling. She's not with Murray. He says he doesn't know where she is, and I believe him. We need to stop any attempt she makes to leave the country if she hasn't done so already. Can you get the word out?"

"Your team needs to initiate an international warrant through Interpol. We can alert US passport control here, at the airport and harbors, but that Interpol warrant is the key. I just hope she's still here and not back in the States."

THIRTY-ONE

Dillon pulled into the parking spot in his front garden and hurried to the door, hoping Lucifer had been able to contain himself since he was last let out in the early morning. He could have taken his time. He unlocked the door then pushed it open. Lucifer was nowhere to be seen, but the evidence he was home lay right at the door. As Dillon opened the door, he smeared the evidence across the small floor mat just inside on the front hall floor. Fortunately, it missed the mail that had fallen through the slot and was lying on the mat, but Lucifer had peed on the mail at least once, making the fact of a miss a bit of a hollow victory.

He was too tired to deal with it at the moment, and he carefully gathered up the floor mat by the edges, careful not to lose the mail or Lucifer's contributions, and set it outside next to the front steps. What remained of Dillon's favorite pillow was scattered up and down the stairs, enough feathers from what had to have been a flock of chickens or geese. He slowly waded through them on his way up the stairs to the bedroom. Lucifer was nowhere to be seen.

He felt the one remaining pillow on the bed. It was cold, which meant Lucifer was hiding somewhere. He didn't feel he had the energy to look, and he had to get up in just a few hours and drive down to Wexford, so he set his alarm clock, added his clothes to the ever-growing pile on the floor, climbed into bed and promptly fell asleep.

The alarm clock seemed to go off a minute later. It was just after four in the morning. Lucifer was curled up on the far corner of the bed and opened one eye with a look that suggested Dillon could turn off the alarm any time now.

Dillon dressed in jeans and a rugby jersey from the pile of clothes on the floor, then gently shook Lucifer awake. He slowly jumped off the bed then stretched, keeping an eye on Dillon as he did so.

"Come on, let's go outside. Are we still friends?"

Lucifer gave no real indication that the friendship was still intact, although he did head down the stairs. Dillon opened the front door, Lucifer took one step, then stopped and looked at the floor mat lying outside with the still-wet mail and the smeared deposit from last night. He looked up at Dillon, then back to the floor mat. His tail began to wag back and forth as if he suddenly remembered what he'd done yesterday, and wasn't it just hilarious?

He hurried outside, circled a couple of times, then faced Dillon, did his business, and hurried back into the house. He followed Dillon into the kitchen. Dillon got the coffee going, filled Lucifer's food and water dish, tossed him a milk bone in the hope the two of them would remain friends, then filled a travel mug with coffee and headed out the door.

Traffic was virtually nonexistent on the way into Dublin city center, and William Street South, Murray's street, was devoid of all but one car, which was clamped. There was no foot traffic. There was someone sleeping in a ratty sleeping bag just two doors down, and Dillon quietly closed his car door so as not to wake him.

Up above on the second floor of the building, the light was on in what looked to be Murray's apartment. Dillon rang the intercom button for Murray's unit, and a moment later, he answered.

"That you?"

"Yeah. Come on down and let's get going," Dillon said.

"Be right there."

A minute later, the door opened, and Murray stepped out. His face and indeed his entire head appeared to have been freshly shaven. A cloud of aftershave drifted over Dillon and enveloped him like a poison gas. He was dressed in leather, black leather, all leather, nothing but leather. He wore a black leather vest with three silver buttons, no shirt. Skin-tight black leather pants with silver zippers on either leg running from mid-calf down to his ankles. He wore black leather cowboy boots, actually snake or alligator skin, with silver toe caps and heels.

"You like?" Murray asked, then slowly turned around with his arms outstretched so Dillon could get the benefit of a 360-degree view.

"You sleep in that? And who the hell is this?" Dillon asked, referring to a guy just stepping out of the door behind Murray. He had two square, black nylon bags hanging by a strap from either shoulder, but other than that and his association with Murray, he appeared more or less to be normal.

"Marshal Dillon, meet the famous Tim Greeley, photographer extraordinaire."

"Photographer?"

"The Marshal goes by Dildo," Murray laughed.

"No I don't, and we're not bringing a photographer, for God's sake. No offense, what'd he say your name was?"

"Greeley, Tim Greeley."

"Sorry, but we're not bringing a photographer. This isn't some fashion shoot. Where in the hell did you get that outfit, by the way? And that aftershave, God, did you swim in it? We'll have to drive with the windows down. No, sorry, but the male model and I have to get going. Get in the car, Murray."

"Not unless Tim's going. He doesn't go, I don't go, and well, then you won't know where to go. Which means you may never find the bullets."

"They're actually shell casings."

"Whatever. You may never find them, and didn't you say you were in a hurry?"

"I don't have time to—"

"Actually, if I might interject," Greeley said. "I've done some crime scene shoots for both the Garda as well as solicitors defending clients from time to time. I've never photographed a murder scene. But wouldn't it make sense to have photos of this scene? Otherwise, you risk the possibility of your testimony being thrown out on the grounds of hearsay."

Dillon considered that for a moment, grudgingly admitted it actually made sense, good sense as a matter of fact, then said, "Okay, hop in, but we're not making this a fashion photoshoot. I need to collect this evidence and get back up here to Dublin as soon as possible."

"Wouldn't dream of getting in your way." Greeley smiled.

Murray gave the thumbs-up, then carefully climbed into the front seat. You could hear his leather pants crinkling and crackling as he slithered into the passenger seat. Dillon hurried around to the driver's side, shaking his head. Suel was going to go crazy.

"Buckle up and crack open a window, or my eyes are going to start watering with all that aftershave," Dillon said once he'd climbed in.

Greeley had already opened one of his camera bags and was busy putting a lens on a camera that looked more like a sniper's scope. "So you're a Marshal back in the States, and you're over here working with the Garda?"

"Yeah, something like that."

"Timmy," Murray said. "Try not to get any shots with my gut hanging out, that'll can any publicity options. You can Photoshop whatever you shoot, right?"

"You are not Photoshopping anything, it'll get thrown right out of court," Dillon said.

"Yeah, whatever," Murray said, then glared at Dillon. "Nothing showing my gut, and I've got a great set of buns, so get some nice ass shots, the ladies always love that."

Greeley didn't reply, but opened his other camera bag and attached a different lens to that camera.

Dillon headed out of the city center toward the M11 motorway and Wexford. It was going to be a long morning.

THIRTY-TWO

Murray hadn't been kidding when he said it was a good two hours to where they were going. It was actually two hours to where the bus had dropped him off, and then another twenty minutes to his cousin's farm.

"I'm thinking we might stop at Kevin's house for a tea, and I should probably use the loo before we head out to the field. Need to freshen up and check myself in the mirror," Murray said, breaking the silence in the car that had existed for the better part of two hours. His voice woke Greeley up in the back seat, and he yawned and stretched.

"We don't have time for any tea," Dillon said.

"Might make you a little less crabby."

"You want to walk back to Dublin?"

"All right, just a suggestion, no need to get…Oh, here at the top of this little hill, you're going to want to take a right."

Dillon took a right turn at the top of the hill onto a narrow country lane. A long hedge lined one side of the road. The other side had what appeared to be an endless stone wall. On the far side of the stone wall was a field of purple flowers.

"They grow flowers out here?"

Murray half-laughed, "Flowers, are you kidding? Wexford is known for its lavender. That's what all the purple is, lavender. Kevin grows lavender, has a couple of fields of the stuff, and well, of course, potatoes. The woman he just married, I guess his wife now, she's involved in some local group. They market the stuff. They make soaps, sprays, bath oils. They're starting to get into a couple of specialty shops up in Dublin now. And she works, she— Oh wait, now there's a tinchy little road up here. See where that tree is, you'll need to take a left there."

Dillon turned after a large dead tree standing just inside another stone wall. The lane they'd been driving on was no wider than maybe a car and a half. The one he had just turned onto would barely qualify as a narrow driveway back in the States. The pavement in places had virtually disappeared, and Dillon had to slow to almost a crawl.

"Now it's just on the far side of those trees. See up ahead on the right-hand side? With any luck, the glass from the bottle should be on top of the wall and wait, stop, there it is. Back up, back up a bit. Yeah, see it? Fecking aye, just like we left it. Timmy, best get a shot of me with the glass. I'll just—"

"Wait a minute, just hold on," Dillon said. "Tim, can we start with you getting shots of the area? Photograph on both sides of the wall and from different angles. Now once he's done taking the photos, let's go over the wall down there a way so as not to disturb anything. When we finally go to where you think the casings are, I want you to follow me. Step where I step. Got it?"

Both Murray and Greeley nodded.

"Okay, let's go. I've got some equipment in the trunk I need to get. Let me go first, always."

"God, Mr. Tight Control, okay, okay," Murray said, then carefully climbed out of the car so as not to damage his skin-tight leather pants.

Dillon opened the trunk of the car, pulled out a box full of large brown paper bags with a plastic window. The bags were labeled in blue with the words "POLICE" and "EVIDENCE" on either side of the plastic window.

"Now, no one is to touch anything except me," Dillon said.

"I know, I know. God, how many times do you have to—"

"Here, make yourself useful," Dillon said and handed Murray a series of small, yellow plastic pieces looking like little tents with numbers on them. "We'll mark where we find the casings first, then photograph them in position."

They waited while Greeley photographed the wall and the broken bottle from different angles. He finished by taking shots of the narrow lane they'd driven down.

"You going to have enough film?" Dillon asked.

Greeley smiled and said, "It's all digital nowadays."

"Oh, yeah."

They walked down the lane a good fifty feet to a low point in the wall and climbed over. Murray brushed a portion of pavement clear of sand. He pulled the skin-tight leather pants down to his thighs, then sat down and pulled the pants completely off. He climbed over the wall wearing just his boots, red boxers, and the leather vest. He ran to catch up to Dillon, then the two of them waited while Greeley photographed the area from a variety of angles. While they waited, Murray carefully inched the leather pants back on and up his thighs.

When Greeley had finished, he gave Dillon a nod. Murray pointed out the general area where he thought Fiona had stood and fired. Dillon carefully approached and quickly spotted first one and then two other spent cartridges. They were silver, rimless, and appeared to be identical to the cartridge that had been collected next to the beer barrels in Dame Lane. Dillon took the yellow plastic tents from Murray and, in short order, had six of them placed next to the spent cartridges. He had Greeley photograph the cartridges from multiple angles.

When Greeley finished photographing, Dillon motioned Murray forward and had Greeley photograph him from different angles. Dillon opened up one of the evidence bags and handed Murray a metal tool that looked like a screwdriver.

"Place that inside the cartridge and then drop it in the bag. Don't touch the cartridge. And here, put these on," he said and handed Murray a pair of blue latex gloves. "We'll collect all six casings. Each one goes in a separate bag. Greeley, you get shots of Murray collecting the evidence."

Murray immediately began to pose with a serious, discerning look on his face. He dropped each silver cartridge into a separate evidence bag. All the while, Greeley kept clicking his camera, shooting images.

Once the cartridges had been gathered, Dillon approached the wall and examined the wine bottle. Most of the neck of the bottle was still intact, and he had Greeley take a number of photos. He had Murray carefully place the pieces of the bottle into more evidence bags, always grasping the bottle fragments by the outside edges or, in the case of the neck of the bottle, using the tool he had supplied. Greeley clicked away with his camera.

The entire process took about forty-five minutes. They were just about ready to leave when Murray said, "Hey, over there. I think it's her thong. She couldn't find it when we left, and we were laughing about that for a couple of days."

He pointed toward the wall, maybe ten feet away, but Dillon couldn't see anything. He stepped closer to Murray and then, following exactly where Murray pointed, looked for a long moment, and suddenly there it was, a small blue article halfway rolled up and lying against the base of the stone wall. The stone just above it hung out maybe two inches further than the course below. It was easy to see how she could have missed it.

Greeley first photographed the area, then took a number of shots of Murray collecting the evidence. In short order, they were back in the car, after a half-dozen more photos of Murray loading the evidence bags into the trunk. Then Dillon carefully reversed down the narrow lane, and they headed back to Dublin.

THIRTY-THREE

They had just pulled off the M11 and onto a Dublin street when Dillon's phone rang. He pulled over to the curb and answered.

"Dillon," Suel shouted the moment Dillon answered.

"What's up?"

"I think we've got her."

"Fiona O'Sullivan?"

"What's the bitch saying about me?" Murray said from the passenger seat.

"Who the hell was that?" Suel asked.

"Enda Murray. We're back from gathering spent cartridges and the shattered wine bottle. Guess what else we got? A—"

"That can wait. We just got confirmation she's here at Trinity, with the old roommates from a few months back. The authorities, with Bergman's help, issued an international warrant, so she won't be able to clear passport control. I've got a team here now. We're just waiting for the okay to go in and get her out of the room."

"Can you hold on for just ten minutes? We can be there and…"

"I've got two people keeping an eye on the room. McCabe is talking with the school officials just now. We're cooling our heels in two Garda vans in a parking area just off Nassau Street, waiting for the okay. You know where the Trinity Arts building is?"

Dillon pulled the phone away from his ear and said, "Either of you know where the Arts Building is off Nassau Street at Trinity?"

"That would be the back of the building," Greeley said.

"You need to get down to Pearse Street," said Murray. He was still wearing the blue latex gloves. "Take that around the campus to Nassau Street. There's a small parking lot in the back. Ten, fifteen minutes we can get there. That's probably where they are, in that little parking lot."

"We're on the way," Dillon said then waited for a car to pass before he took off, accelerating.

"Oh please, let me arrest her. This will be so great. 'Your party days are over, Fiona,'" Murray said, striking a TV pose. "You can get all this, Timmy," he said to Greeley. "We can sell this to the newspapers, no, wait, a movie, get it? It'll be fecking Hollywood, lads."

"No way that's happening," Dillon said. "You shouldn't even be here in the first place, so you two are staying in the car. Got it? Besides, she's armed and dangerous and apparently a pretty good shot."

"Hmmm-mmm, maybe you've got a point," Murray said.

With Dillon driving, running three or four stop lights, they made the trip in eight minutes and pulled in behind the two Garda vans taking up most of the parking lot. The cars were a bright fluorescent yellow-green with double doors in the back, and the words "GARDA" in large blue letters on the sides. There were flashing lights mounted on top of each vehicle, but they were currently turned off.

Suel stood behind one of the vans, talking to a Guard dressed all in black and wearing a heavy flak vest. They both glared at the car as Dillon pulled in, but Suel smiled once he recognized Dillon behind the wheel and said something to the guy in the flak vest.

"Perfect timing. We're about to head over. They're on the far side of campus, a place called Goldsmith Hall. McCabe just called with the approval. We'll drive over once you get your wanker-mobile out of the parking lot."

"Nice bit of detailing." The guy in the flak vest smiled and nodded at the spray-painted "Wanker" on the driver's door.

"Let me back up, and I'll block traffic so you can get out," Dillon said and climbed back in the car. He backed onto the street, blocking a lane of traffic. Two horns immediately sounded behind him. One of the drivers leaned on the horn and didn't stop.

"Want me to go deal with that?" Murray said.

"No, let's just stay focused, which in your case means stay in the damn car. We're going around to Gold-smith Hall. God, I wish that jackass behind us would lay off the horn."

With that, the horn stopped as the two large Garda vehicles drove out of the parking lot. Dillon followed closely behind the second vehicle.

"This is liable to go quickly. I want you two to stay in the car," Dillon said as they followed the Garda vans around a corner. A minute later, they stopped, and the back doors on the van in front of them burst open. Damn near a platoon of men dressed all in black, wearing flak vests and carrying automatic weapons, hurried out and around the vans.

Dillon jumped out of the car, shouted, "Stay put," at Murray and Greeley, and then ran to catch up with the group charging toward the front door of the building. As he ran, he was draping an ID card around his neck.

Murray and Greeley waited a good fifteen seconds before they followed behind.

Four men, all dressed in black, wearing flak vests and armed, charged across the street. They ran up a stair-case, then came back across the street in an enclosed walkway, entering Goldsmith Hall on the second floor. The rest of the group, over a dozen, all in black with flak vests and armed, charged through the front doors of the building. Dillon and Suel followed close behind. Murray and Greeley followed just a few feet behind them.

There were screams and shouts of shocked surprise in the lobby of the building as the group charged down a hallway. They took a staircase up to the second floor and then down a long hallway. They met up with the group of four men already positioned in the second-floor hall, two kneeling down against the wall on either side of a doorway. Half the group quietly hurried past the door until there were ten armed men positioned on either side. The guy who'd been standing in the parking lot with Suel when Dillon had first pulled up now waved Suel forward.

They spoke briefly. Suel nodded, then stepped forward and knocked on the door to the room, calling out, "Housekeeping," as he did so. He knocked a second time. The door opened, and everyone burst in. High-pitched screams came from inside the apartment, followed by men shouting, "Down on the floor. Get down. Get down".

It was all over in just a brief moment. Dillon, Murray, and Greeley followed in after the assault force. Greeley shot pictures as fast as he could. Murray, still wearing the blue latex gloves, edged his way toward the front and posed.

Dillon was in the background of the photos, saying something official to a slight, dark-haired woman lying on the floor while Suel clapped a pair of handcuffs on her behind her back.

Three young women stood off to the side with shocked looks on their faces. One of them continued eating a sandwich. What looked like a small, black backpack lay on the floor, and just peeping out from the top of the backpack was the handgrip of a small pink pistol.

Murray quickly turned around and gave Greeley a nod, then struck another pose. Greeley continued taking pictures, moving around Murray to get as many armed men as possible in the background. For his part, Murray unbuttoned his vest, sucked in his stomach, puffed out his chest and crossed his arms.

Greeley kept clicking his camera until Dillon stepped over and said, "Knock that shit off, the both of you."

As Fiona O'Sullivan was led out of the small apartment by Suel and McCabe, her eyes widened at the sight of Murray and his leather outfit. "You, you miserable, low, worse than a total plonker, son of a...."

"Justice has been served. You're under arrest. I knew I'd have the last laugh," Murray said and struck a pose. Greeley's camera started clicking. "Go ahead, get her out of here," Murray said to McCabe, who got a very puzzled look on his face as he led Fiona out the door and down the hall.

"I think it's time to leave," Dillon said.

"This is even better than I ever could have hoped," Murray said and gave Greeley a high five slap.

"Let's get the two of you out of here before they confiscate that camera," Dillon said under his breath.

"Oh yeah, right, right," Murray said and hurried out
the door.

Two weeks later and McCabe still hadn't completely calmed down. Dillon had spent the better part of the morning in McCabe's office, getting reamed out four ways to Sunday for possibly contaminating evidence with the presence of Greeley and Murray at the scene. At least until Dillon explained that it was Murray who spotted the thong, which conclusively linked Fiona O'Sullivan to the site along with the spent casings that matched the one found at the crime scene.

"But the newspaper article and this, this apparent movie deal? Hollywood, for God's sake. A television show with this Murray plonker as the star?"

"Yeah, not the best situation, at least initially, I admit. But because of all this, Fiona O'Sullivan pled guilty to the murder. We avoided a costly trial. She'll be sentenced. The family recovered the prize guitar, and they can at least attempt to get on with their lives. You've got the government off your back, and Murray almost out of the country."

"But those photographs, they make it appear like you were nothing more than a driver to get this idiot on the scene. And that outfit, the bollocks is strutting around in that leather costume with the latex gloves. What in God's name?"

"And, because of that, the newspaper story—"

"Story? The damn thing was a front page exclusive in the bloody Sunday edition," McCabe said, and half-threw the newspaper across the desk in Dillon's direction.

"And because of that, he's leaving for the States tomorrow, flying to Los Angeles and, I hasten to add, out of your hair. Not to mention some pretty good press for the department."

"Good press? God," McCabe said and gradually adjusted his vision to stare out the window. "What an absolute clusterfuck. And you're sure this Murray is leaving the country? The bollocks sent me an invitation to some dreadful event this evening. I don't intend to reply."

"Oh yeah, that's his going-away party. I'm attending it this evening at—"

"You're what?" McCabe half-shouted.

"Murray's, umm, going-away party. It's this evening, and I was invited, too. I thought, you know, make a brief appearance, wish him well, make sure he's leaving the country, and then flee the scene. Might be a bit of good public relations, sir. Bound to be reporters and news people there."

"God, I suppose you'll be wearing black leather. All right, go on, get out of my sight. I don't want to hear any more about it, and I certainly do not want to read about it in the newspaper tomorrow. Now, go on, get out," McCabe said, then waved his hand dismissively.

* * *

Jynx was playing, and Murray was on stage dressed in his leather outfit, the vest, skin-tight pants, the snake-skin boots, or whatever they were, only tonight he was wearing a Garda baseball cap, oh yeah, and the blue latex gloves. God only knew where he'd gotten the cap. They were all crowded into the Dew Drop, a pub Murray apparently frequented and, based on the crowd tonight, a place only too happy to host. Fans were six deep at the bar, waving twenty-euro notes for pints and drinks. The six bartenders couldn't keep up. The stage was mobbed by women screaming and exposing themselves while Murray and Jynx played.

Dillon was seated at a table with Bergman and Suel. McCabe, looking disgusted and checking his watch, was seated next to Suel.

Joe Carroll from the Musician's Union was playing onstage with Jynx, and Tim Greeley was up there as well, taking lots of pictures. Dillon noticed Margaret Kinney, the redhead from Murray's apartment, screaming up at the front of the stage, waving at Murray.

"Oh, this is so exciting." Claire leaned forward with a shrug and squeezed Dillon's thigh. "Don't mind saying, I hated the plonker when he was living down the hall from me. Then I wake up Sunday morning, and he's some kind of hero on the front page of the paper and headed to Hollywood to be a star. Who knew?"

"Yeah, that more or less seems to be everyone's reaction."

"Well—" She glanced around, then leaned in even closer. "Well, it's all because of you, and I, for one, will be glad to see the backside of him. Well done, you, Marshal Dillon. I wonder how I can ever pay you back," she said, then raised her eyebrows and smiled. "What say we maybe finish these pints and head back to my place?"

Dillon hoisted his half-filled glass of Guinness and gulped it down, then set the empty glass on the table and said, "I'm ready."

The End

Thank you for taking the time to read <u>Silver Bullet</u>, the fourth book in the Jack Dillon Dublin Tales series. Since I'm indie published reviews help. If you enjoyed the read please feel free to take a moment and leave a review. Even if it's just a sentence or two it really, really helps, many thanks in advance and best to you and yours...

Don't miss the following sample of the fifth book in the Jack Dillon Dublin Tales series, <u>Fair City Blues</u>.

PROLOGUE

rkady Sokolov was down on his knees next to the body. He pulled and tugged on the gold ring with the blue stone, but it remained on the finger. The finger was swollen, and he was unable to turn the ring, let alone pull it off. In frustration, he picked up the red-handled saw, shoved the battery into the base of the handle, set the blade against the finger, and cut it off in less than a second.

"I'm not going to tell you again, stop wasting my time, and get that taken care of, we've got a long night ahead of us," Yakov Gulin said. As he spoke in Russian, he kicked Arkady on the back of his shoulder lurching him forward.

Yakov had a low brow on his shaved head, made to appear even lower due to his one thick, bushy eyebrow. He towered over Arkady, who had been driving him crazy for the better part of the night. *Once this was over*, Yakov thought, *Arkady Sokolov just might be put to rest, too*.

"Just a little souvenir, it isn't every night—"

"I'll give you a souvenir, something to remember me by if you don't get that taken care of in the next five minutes. Now, I'm going to get the car. I'll expect the hands in that bag by the time I get back."

"Yes, sir," Arkady said, smiled his idiot grin then waved the saw in a sort of mock salute. Blood from the blade flew in all directions, and he reflexively put his hand up to shield from the spray, in the process running the palm of his hand across the saw blade and slicing it open.

"You fool. We put the plastic on the floor for a damn good reason. Now either you start paying attention to what in the hell you're doing, or as God is my witness, you're going to find yourself the next one stretched out on the floor. Tie a rag around that to stop the bleeding. I'll be back in four and a half minutes, and God help you if you keep me waiting," Yakov shouted, then stormed out of the room.

Arkady watched him head out the door, then gave him the finger once the door was closed and he wouldn't see. He pulled a rag stained with paint and grease off the workbench and wrapped it around his hand, then got down to business. He cut the right hand off at the wrist, then the left, and tossed them both into the plastic bag. He picked up the finger and easily pried the ring off at the base, dropped the finger into the white plastic shopping bag, and pocketed the gold ring. Blood from his hand began to seep through the rag, and he held it over the open plastic bag. Blood dripped into the bag as he folded the soiled rag over four or five times and tied it using just his right hand, grabbing one end of the rag with thumb and forefinger, the other end with his teeth, and pulling the knot tight. He shook his head to regain his bearings, the vodka from earlier in the night, apparently still having an effect.

He placed the saw blade against the neck, turned his head, so he didn't have to look, then pulled the trigger on the saw and dragged his way across. The blade paused for a moment, held up on bone, which caused Arkady to look. He took hold of the saw with both hands, forcing it through the upper spine until the head rolled off to the side.

That had always been the most difficult part, the victim's spine, and he took a deep breath, swallowed down whatever was in the process of rising up from his stomach, and set the saw off to the side.

The blonde hair was close-cropped, forcing Arkady to place both hands on either side of the head and lift it into the plastic bag. Although it certainly wasn't his first time, he was always more than a little surprised at the weight. The head landed in the bag with a soggy-sounding plop. Arkady quickly twisted the bag closed, letting the air out as he did so, then tied the end in a loose knot.

He grabbed the saw, stepped over to the industrial sink, rinsed off the blade, then took a sponge and wiped off the saw. He placed his hands beneath the armpits and lifted the headless corpse from under the arms, essentially folding it in half, then placed his knee against the back to hold it place while he cautiously rolled the plastic around the body. He worked carefully, making sure the blood didn't flow onto the floor before he taped the plastic closed. He'd just set the roll of tape down when the door opened.

"Are you ready?" Yakov growled as he stepped back into the room.

Arkady nodded, lifted up the white plastic bag containing the head and hands. "It's all in here."

Yakov gave an exasperated sigh and shook his head. "Do you ever listen? Idiot, do I have to do everything? Not in the same bag. Put the bastard's skull in a separate bag, and crush it, takes up less room that way. There's a hammer on the workbench. I'll be back in a moment."

Arkady watched him as he left the room. Once out the door, he gave him the finger again. His injured hand throbbed as he thrust his middle finger into the air, and he cursed and hoped Yakov's mother was raped by a dog, a large dog. He took a green trash bag from the roll on the workbench, opened it, and set it on the floor. He untied the loose knot in the bag with the hands and finger, took hold of the skull by the tops of the ears, and pulled it out. He laid the skull in the green trash bag, then placed a canvas drop cloth over the bag, turned the hammer sideways, and began to pummel the skull, gradually breaking it down into smaller and smaller sections. He lifted the canvas drop cloth a half-dozen times to check his progress, before continuing to pummel, until eventually, the trash bag contained nothing more than a bony sort of stew.

ONE

oira Sweeney was the focus of Dillon's comment, not that Detective Chief Inspector McCabe seemed the least bit interested. "Well then, Marshal Dillon, my first thought is that it might behoove you to stop wasting your time and mine as well. Would it not be wise to simply get behind the wheel of your vehicle and depart, with all due haste, to the office of the state pathologist and view the body?"

"I'm just thinking, unidentified, apparently floating in the Royal Canal for some time, resting peacefully on a refrigerated shelf. I'm wondering if it couldn't wait until morning? Clearly, it's not going anywhere, and as I mentioned, I have an early dinner reservation this evening at six."

It was more than just a dinner reservation. This was to be the all important third date. He'd met Moira at a party after a rugby match a few weeks back, Ireland playing England in the Six Nations tournament. A great tournament, Ireland, England, Scotland, Wales, France and Italy, with any team on any day capable of winning. Unfortunately, the match that day had gone to England, winning nine to six. But he'd met Moira at the after party, so all had not been lost. They'd hooked up in a pub the following Friday with friends, the two of them just getting to know one another a little better. They'd gone to O'Donaghue's pub the following Sunday night to listen to session music, where she gave him the perfunctory 'Have a nice week,' then headed home, alone, just to prove she wasn't a slut. Tonight was to be the all important date number three, where, since proving she wasn't that type of girl last week, she could freely hop in the sack with Dillon after dinner tonight.

"Your dinner reservation can be put back by an hour, in fact, less than that if you'd make yourself scarce and get out of my office. Now, I want you there this evening, so you'll be able to provide a full report first thing in the morning. I've got a meeting at nine, and I want you standing tall." McCabe pointed to the floor in front of his desk where Dillon was now standing. "I want you in here tomorrow morning, no later than one minute past eight. Questions?"

"No, sir. On my way," Dillon said, trying to sound positive and failing miserably.

He fled McCabe's office, hurried out to his car, and raced out of the parking lot.

He needn't have hurried. It was close to five in the evening and the Dublin rush hour was in full swing. Fifteen minutes later he was in bumper to bumper traffic that wasn't going anywhere along Drumcondra Road. People on foot had been passing him for the last ten minutes. Now they were all blocks ahead of him, and he was still moving by inches, three lanes of rush hour traffic with buses merging down to just one outside the Cat and Cage pub. Add to that the poorly timed stoplights along the way and he was late, late, late. He tried to call Moira a half dozen times but kept getting dumped into her voicemail.

He finally made it up to the Office of the State Pathologist, turned onto Griffith Avenue, pulled up onto the boulevard in front of someone's house and parked. Traffic remained heavy and he had to cross with the light, which took another three or four minutes. It was ten minutes before six, no way was he going to meet Moira on time. He called her again as a car without its blinker flashing leaned on the horn as Dillon ran across the street. He was in too much of a hurry to stop and kick out the man's headlights. Besides, he was dumped into her voicemail again, so it really didn't matter.

He entered the grounds through the wrought-iron gate. A rectangular grey granite stone just next to the sidewalk read "Marbhlann Chathair Bhaile Atha Cliath & Oifig an Phaiteolai Stáit," and below that, in slightly smaller letters the English translation, "Dublin City Mortuary & Office of the State Pathologist." Dillon rang the after-hours bell, explained who he was to the voice that came across on the speaker, then waited.

"Working late, are we?" the man clad in blue hospital scrubs, Brian McFadden, asked when he opened the door a few minutes later.

"No rest for the wicked, Brian," Dillon replied, then stepped in and followed Brian down the long hallway to the rear of the building. Framed watercolor street images of Dublin hung on both sides of the off-white hallway. He could see into most of the offices through windows next to the office doors. With one exception, all the offices were empty. They walked past the labs and the examination rooms. At this hour, it was quiet, deathly quiet, as he followed Brian into the rear storage area.

Brian walked along the wall of steel drawers, stacked five high and twenty long, large enough to hold a hundred bodies. Each drawer was numbered.

"Ahhh, here we are," Brian said, then placed a key into the lock next to the handle and pulled the drawer open. "Bit of a rough one, this is. Been in the water for at least two weeks," he said, pulling the drawer open. "We've him frozen, to slow down the decomposition."

The naked form in front of Dillon had apparently been a blonde man. The corpse was headless, and it took Dillon a moment to run his eyes back and forth over the body before he realized the hands were missing, too.

"Not much to go on," Brian said casually as if he were describing a used car. "The hands and head appear to have been removed by some powered instrument. An educated guess, I'd say a saw. Here's the reason McCabe probably decided to spice up the end of your day. Come on over to this side," he said, slipping on a pair of green latex gloves as Dillon walked around the open drawer.

When he came around and stepped beside him, Brian gave a nod, then placed his hands beneath the shoulder of the corpse and lifted. The entire body rose like a large wooden plank, exposing a tattoo covering the left shoulder blade. It was large, maybe eight inches high, an eagle, globe, and anchor, the official emblem of the United States Marine Corp. Draped across the globe was a banner that read, "Fallujah 2004."

"That mean anything to you?" Brian asked.

"Whoever he is, it's a pretty good guess he was a Marine, and he fought in Iraq. Fallujah was a hell of an ongoing battle. If he was there, he saw more than his fair share of action."

"Interesting," Brian said, sounding anything but interested. "Let me show you the other side."

They walked back around to the other side of the open drawer. Brian gave a grunt as he lifted the body again, exposing a wound from roughly the hip all the way up to the shoulder.

Dillon bent down for a closer look, then said, "What do you make of it?"

"It happened in the water, after death. I'm thinking it may be the reason he was discovered. Something, probably a large vessel, scrapped against him, just conjecture here, but probably loosening him from whatever was holding him beneath the surface. Maybe chains or rope, although there really aren't any telltale signs of that on the body. Interestingly we did recover some synthetic threads along this abrasion. Possibly a windbreaker or a jacket that was covering him."

"Did he have clothing?"

"Yes. It's still here, although I don't know that there's anything to be learned. I've been waiting for the Garda to pick them up. Probably good they didn't make it today, and you can still examine them. There was nothing related to the synthetic threads we recovered from the abrasion. Come on, we can take a look," Brian said as he lowered the body back onto the shelf and shoved the drawer closed.

TWO

The clothing was contained in clear plastic bags labeled "evidence." A separate bag for each item of clothing. The name "Doe, John" and a reference number were written on both bags sitting on the top shelf of a metal, four-wheeled cart parked in the corner of the lab.

"Help yourself," Brian said. "My estimate is a minimum of a couple of weeks, at least in the Royal Canal. Feel free to handle them. There's a box of gloves on the second shelf of that cart. While you're looking, I'll just send an email, McCabe wanted to be kept in the loop when you arrived. Sounds like he's got you on a short leash."

"I think he lives in fear of those Russian bastards making another attempt on me. Not that he really cares, I think it's more a matter of he doesn't want to face the paperwork."

Brian laughed, then headed into his office. Dillon pulled two latex gloves from the box, slipped them on then opened the evidence bag. A sort of musty scent immediately met him as he pulled a pair of black jeans from the bag. The pockets were empty, and he held the jeans out at arm's length in front of him, turning them from front to back. He examined the pockets, the fly, and the waistband, looking for any defining label, but didn't see one. Four bits of thread were on the back, along the right side of the waist, where a label might traditionally be on a pair of jeans. Most likely, the label had been pulled off. He folded the jeans and placed them back in the bag, then opened the second bag, a pair of boxers, black cotton socks, and a black t-shirt. Again no tags on the shirt, although the frayed remnants of a tag remained on the back of the t-shirt. The back of the t-shirt along one side had a series of holes running from the bottom up to the shoulder that appeared to correspond with the long abrasion on the body. Had the tags been removed by the owner? Simply worn off? Or was someone being careful to remove all identifiable evidence? The shoes were a pair of black Nikes, but other than the Nike Swoosh, there were no identifiable marks, although they were clearly worn and not new.

"What do you think?" Brian asked, stepping out of his office. He held a mug of tea, took a sip, and grimaced. "Oh, God, but this tea is desperate."

"I think these could have been purchased just about anywhere, either in the EU or in the States. Nothing resembling a tag remains on anything, although the t-shirt and the jeans appear to have been tagged initially."

"We did find a euro in the small front pocket? You know, that little one, for coins or maybe a pocket watch."

"A euro?"

"Yeah. Irish, dated 2012, not that the year means anything or the fact it was Irish."

"Go back to those tags for a minute. Think they were just worn off?"

"Possibly, but I think it's more likely someone removed them. The next question is was it our friend in there on the shelf or whoever deposited him in the canal?"

"You send McCabe the email so he can rest easy tonight?" Dillon said.

"Just did. I'm not sure he'll rest easy, but at least he knows you're here."

"Do you know where that body was found?" Dillon said.

"Yeah, the Royal Canal. That's the plastic the body was wrapped in, that bag on the bottom shelf." Brian indicated the cart, and for the first time, Dillon noticed the clear plastic neatly folded into another evidence bag. "The plastic is heavy-duty, something maybe a contractor would use, the sort of thing you'd find on a construction site. Blood remnants would seem to indicate they laid the plastic on a floor, placed the body on the plastic, decapitated and removed the hands on your man, then rolled him up in the plastic and sent the entire package to the bottom of the canal."

"Anything from the plastic?"

"Not so much, other than confirmation it had been around the body." Brian shook his head. "There's damage along a portion of the plastic consistent with the damage along the victim's back, something apparently tearing against the corpse. It's one of but not the only reason, I'm estimating time in the water at a minimum of two weeks. There was something weighing down the body, stones, chains, something, but over time as decomposition started and the body filled with gas it rose to the surface. It would have risen sooner if the head had been left in place. The gas from decomposition…."

"I get it," Dillon said. "So you've not found the chains or stones or whatever had weighed the body down?"

"Right. Eventually, the body rose, floated some distance away, maybe quite some distance, before it was spotted."

"Who spotted it?"

"A couple, husband and wife, they were out for a stroll, pushing a granddaughter in a stroller along the canal. Have you walked along there, the Royal Canal?"

"No. Been past it uncountable times, but, no, I've never actually walked there. You got some kind of a map to show me where the body was found?"

"Amazingly, I do," Brian said, then stepped over to a stainless steel sink and dumped the remainder of his tea down the drain. "Step into my lair," he said and went back to his office. He opened an upholstered panel attached to a shelf mounted on the wall, fingered his way through a number of documents, then pulled out a tourist map of central Dublin and spread it open on his desk.

"This area," he said, circling an upper portion of the map with his finger, "is known as Cross Guns. This is Phibsborough Road, here. Do you know it?"

"I'm past there almost every day. The Brian Boru pub is just about here?" Dillon said and pointed.

"Yeah, exactly. About a hundred paces from the pub heading down Phibsborough Road toward the city center is a business called Des Kelly's. They sell beds, carpet, floor laminate."

"Yeah, I've seen the place."

"You take a turn into Des Kelly's, and the entrance to the canal is right there. There's a paved path wide enough for a car, and you can drive almost to where the body was found. Lock number seven was where it was spotted, literally up against the gate. You can't quite drive there without the Waterway Assistance. They'd have to unlock the iron barriers set across the path. They allow pedestrian and bicycle traffic only, no cars from that point forward. It's somewhat isolated, although it's fairly well traveled with local foot traffic and cyclists."

Dillon knew exactly where he was talking about. "I can be there tomorrow and check it out."

"Fancy a pint? I've time for just the one," Brian said.

"Yeah, I can fit that…Oh, Christ."

"Problem?"

"I was supposed to meet a friend for dinner." He glanced at the large clock on the wall, mounted up by the ceiling. "Supposed to meet her over a half-hour ago. God."

"I guess you're about to see if she's the patient sort," Brian laughed as Dillon hurried out of the lab.

He hurried to the lobby, then stepped outside and phoned Moira, only to get dumped into her voicemail again. He swore, then dashed across the street and over to his car.

THREE

Traffic had thinned substantially. That and racing a good twenty miles per hour above the speed limit had Dillon in front of Restaurant Patrick Guilbaud, at just a little after seven, over an hour late for their date. The restaurant was located in a red-brick Georgian building on Upper Merrion St. There was no parking in front, so Dillon drove up onto the sidewalk, set the hazard lights flashing on his car, and hurried up the front steps to the large white door.

He hurried inside, glancing left and right as he approached a smiling woman standing behind a small counter. An open book lay in front of her. A stack of menus, actually long sheets on an elegant grey paper, rested on a table behind her.

"Good evening, sir, and welcome to—" She had a French accent.

"Yes, sorry, but I'm horribly late. I had a reservation for two at six o'clock, and I don't know if my—"

"Oh, so you must be the infamous, Mr. Dillon."

"Yeah. Is she still here?"

"Yes, sir, she's been waiting for you. This way," she said, sounding like she was all too aware of the situation.

He followed the hostess into a long narrow dining room. The room had a high, curved ceiling, which gave it an almost tunnel effect. White linen tablecloths, linen napkins, elegant silver place settings, and the quiet hum of conversation filled the room. As they headed toward the back of the room, Dillon had the feeling a number of people were staring, probably whispering, "Oh look, he's finally here."

He spotted Moira at a table in the far back corner. She was dressed in a silky black sparkly number with spaghetti straps that crossed just below her neck then crossed again on her back. The cups on the dress were absolutely overflowing and made her look all the more sexy. She sipped from her glass of wine, watching as he approached. The look on her face gave nothing away.

"Hi, Moira. Sorry, I'm late. I can explain. I—"

"Sir," the hostess said, pulling a chair out for him.

"What? Oh yeah, thanks, but I think I'll sit over there," he said, taking the seat that happened to be farthest away from Moira, but feeling more comfortable that no one would be seated behind him. He glanced around. "Look, I'm really sorry. Something came up and…."

"Would Monsieur care for something to drink?" the hostess asked.

Dillon glanced over at the wine bottle sitting in the silver bucket next to Moira.

"Yeah, I think maybe I could use a glass of wine."

"Oh, please, allow me," Moira said, then pulled the wine bottle from the bucket, topped off her glass until it was almost filled to the rim, and only a drop remained in the bottle. She half slammed the empty back into the silver bucket and said, "Gee, too bad, I drank it all by myself."

"Oh, umm, that's, that's okay. I think we'll just have another bottle of that wine," Dillon said.

"Yes, of course. Coming right away, sir," the hostess said, then seemed to hurry off just as fast as she could.

Moira took two hearty gulps from her glass while she glared over the rim at Dillon. She took another gulp, then set the glass down.

"Look, sorry I'm late. You're right to be mad. It's just that I tried to call you over a half dozen times, but I kept getting dumped into your voicemail."

"Oh, really?" she said, sounding like she didn't believe him.

"Yes, really. You have your cell here? Is it on?"

She reached over, pulled her purse off the chair next to her, and placed it on the table. Dillon noticed her movements were a little clumsy. She took her cell phone out, fumbled with it and dropped it on the table, then picked it up, pressed a button, and swiped a finger across the screen. She tapped the screen two more times.

"Gee, funny," she said, then held the screen out so he could see it. "This says I didn't get so much as one fecking call from the likes of you."

"What? But that's impossible. Honest, Moira, I was calling. Here, let me try again, maybe something's wrong with your phone." He pulled his cell out, pushed the speed dial number he used to call her, and waited. He could hear the ringing on his phone, but nothing was happening on Moira's phone. He put his phone on speaker so they could both listen.

"So?"

"Can't you hear it ringing? It seems obvious your phone isn't—"

"Hello? Jack, is that you?" a woman's voice said. She didn't sound happy.

"Oh, umm, sorry. I think I really got the wrong number."

"No, you didn't. You've been calling my number almost nonstop for the past two hours. I told you never, ever to call me again. I don't want to hear from you. I do not want to see you, ever. Do you understand? Do not ever—"

He disconnected.

"Sorry about that. Well, crazy me. I, I guess I was calling the wrong number the entire time."

"Gee, amazing, there's another woman who's had just about all she can stand from you? What restaurant did you abandon her in?"

"Look, Moira, something came up at work at the last minute. I was so worried that I'd be late that I made it even worse and then made myself even more late. I'm really, really sorry."

"This is kind of the way it's going to be, isn't it? You're going to always have that one more thing you have to do, and I can just cool my heels while you're doing it, and then when we do go somewhere, you're always looking around to see if someone is going to be behind you."

"It sort of comes with the job. I have to be careful where I—"

"Yeah, maybe. Except it's not like that here, Jack. This is Ireland. We go to a pub, and we may end up talking to people we don't know. We've never seen them before, and we'll never see them again, but they're our best friend for the entire night. You just don't seem to get that."

"I get it. It's just that I'm in a business that's time sensitive, and sometimes—"

"And so apparently that means I can just sit here and drink a bottle of wine all by myself."

"Well, yeah, sometimes. I mean, no, it doesn't mean that, but well, sometimes shit happens."

"Yeah, you're right about the shit," she said and glared. "Right now, what's happening is, I have to go to the loo, so if you'll excuse me," she said and stood up.

Her short dress formed a perfect 'V' in the front, exposing her gorgeous upper thighs, then wrapped around to her fantastic rear. Dillon stared appraisingly as she walked toward the ladies' room, hoping he would be able to get things back on track for the rest of the evening.

"Monsieur," a gentleman said, interrupting Dillon's concentration. He bent over slightly, smiling and holding a bottle of wine in both hands like one might hold a newborn.

"What?"

"The wine, it is what you ordered. No?" he said in a heavy French accent.

"Oh yeah, yeah, sure, that's fine, just fine."

"Very good," he said, then made a production of removing the foil from the top of the bottle and around the neck. He slowly inserted the corkscrew, pulled the cork up, and then, with a second effort, let it pop loudly from the bottle. He twisted the cork off the corkscrew, then placed it upside down next to Dillon to examine.

"Monsieur?" he said, holding the bottle over Dillon's empty glass.

Dillon nodded, then glanced back toward the ladies' room for a moment. No Moira. He turned and looked at his wine glass. Just a small swallow sat in the glass, waiting for Dillon's approval.

"Oh, yeah, I'm sure it's just great. Go ahead, fill me up."

The waiter nodded, filled Dillon's glass, removed the empty bottle from the silver bucket, replaced it with the fresh bottle, and left just as Moira stepped out of the ladies' room.

She looked delicious in her short, sexy dress, and Dillon wondered if he shouldn't just suggest they head back to his place, then quickly decided it might be better to get some food in her and let her calm down.

As she stepped alongside him, he raised his glass of wine and said, "Here's to you, Moira. Thanks for putting up with me."

She stood next to her chair, smiled, raised her glass, and said, "I'll drink to that first part." She took a healthy sip, made two audible gulps, then set her glass back down on the table, threw a cloth object into Dillon's face, and said, "Enjoy yourself tonight," and stormed out of the dining room.

Dillon watched her leave, aware half the people in the restaurant were watching him while the other half watched Moira as she blazed a trail out of the dining room.

He looked down at the silky black cloth she'd thrown in his face. It had a small triangular section with sparkly sequins and was perfumed. He held it up between his thumbs and forefingers for a brief moment before he realized it was her thong.

The woman at the table next to him half-shouted, "Oh, sweet Jaysus."

Dillon took a sip from his wine glass, pretended to remain calm, then signaled the waiter for his check.

"Sir?"

"I think just the check, please."

"But the wine? It is just opened for you."

"Yeah, you can keep it. Just the check, please."

The waiter gave a look suggesting "crazy American's," then hurried away. Dillon stuffed the thong in his pocket, hurriedly emptied his wine glass, and paid the bill.

To be continued . . .

Thanks for taking the time to check out the sample of <u>Fair City Blues</u>, the fifth book in the Jack Dillon Dublin Tales series. Maybe it *can* hurt to ask . . .

BOOKS BY MIKE FARICY
CRIME FICTION FIRSTS

A boxset of the first four books in four crime fiction series:

Russian Roulette; Dev Haskell series
Welcome; Jack Dillon Dublin Tales series
Corridor Man; Corridor Man series
Reduced Ransom! Hot Shot series

The following titles comprise the Dev Haskell series:

Russian Roulette: Case 1
Mr. Swirlee: Case 2
Bite Me: Case 3
Bombshell: Case 4
Tutti Frutti: Case 5
Last Shot: Case 6
Ting-A-Ling: Case 7
Crickett: Case 8
Bulldog: Case 9
Double Trouble: Case 10
Yellow Ribbon: Case 11
Dog Gone: Case 12
Scam Man: Case 13
Foiled: Case 14
What Happens in Vegas… Case 15
Art Hound: Case 16
The Office: Case 17

Star Struck: Case 18
International Incident: Case 19
Guest From Hell: Case 20
Art Attack: Case 21
Mystery Man: Case 22
Bow-Wow Rescue: Case 23
Cold Case: Case 24
Cash Up Front: Case 25
Dream House: Case 26
Alley Katz: Case 27
The Big Gamble: Case 28
Bad to the Bone: Case 29
Silencio!: Case 30
Surprise, Surprise: Case 31
Hit & Run: Case 32
Suspect Santa: Case 33
P.I. Apprentice: Case 34
Rebel Without a Clue: Case 35
Puppy Love: Case 36

The following titles are Dev Haskell novellas:
Dollhouse
The Dance
Pixie
Fore!
Twinkle Toes
(*a Dev Haskell short story*)

The following are Dev Haskell Boxsets:
Dev Haskell Boxset 1-3
Dev Haskell Boxset 4-6
Dev Haskell Boxset 7-9
Dev Haskell Boxset 10-12
Dev Haskell Boxset 13-15
Dev Haskell Boxset 16-18
Dev Haskell Boxset 19-21
Dev Haskell Boxset 22-24
Dev Haskell Boxset 25-27
Dev Haskell Boxset 28-30
Dev Haskell Boxset 1-7
Dev Haskell Boxset 8-14
Dev Haskell Boxset 15-19
Dev Haskell Boxset 20-24
Dev Haskell Boxset 25-29

The following titles comprise the Jack Dillon Dublin Tales series:
Welcome
Jack Dillon Dublin Tale 1
Sweet Dreams
Jack Dillon Dublin Tale 2
Mirror Mirror
Jack Dillon Dublin Tale 3
Silver Bullet
Jack Dillon Dublin Tale 4
Fair City Blues

Jack Dillon Dublin Tale 5
Spade Work
Jack Dillon Dublin Tale 6
Madeline Missing
Jack Dillon Dublin Tale 7
Mistaken Identity
Jack Dillon Dublin Tale 8
Picture Perfect
Jack Dillon Dublin Tale 9
Dublin Moon
Jack Dillon Dublin Tale 10
Mystery Woman
Jack Dillon Dublin Tale 11
Second Chance
Jack Dillon Dublin Tale 12
Payback Brother
Jack Dillon Dublin Tale 13
The Heist
Jack Dillon Dublin Tale 14
Jewels To Kill For
Jack Dillon Dublin Tale 15
Retirement Scheme
Jack Dillon Dublin Tale 16
The Collector
Jack Dillon Dublin Tale 17

Jack Dillon Dublin Tales Boxsets:
Jack Dillon Dublin Tales 1-3
Jack Dillon Dublin Tales 4-6

Jack Dillon Dublin Tales 1-5
Jack Dillon Dublin Tales 1-7
Jack Dillon Dublin Tales 6-10

The following titles comprise the Hotshot series;
Reduced Ransom! Second Edition
Finders Keepers! Second Edition
Bankers Hours Second Edition
Chow Down Second Edition
Moonlight Dance Academy Second Edition
Irish Dukes (Fight Card Series)
written under the pseudonym Jack Tunney

The following titles comprise the Corridor Man series:
Corridor Man
Corridor Man 2: Opportunity knocks
Corridor Man 3: The Dungeon
Corridor Man 4: Dead End
Corridor Man 5: Finger
Corridor Man 6: Exit Strategy
Corridor Man 7: Trunk Music
Corridor Man 8: Birthday Boy
Corridor Man 9: Boss Man
Corridor Man 10: Bye Bye Bobby

Corridor Man novellas:
Corridor Man: Valentine
Corridor Man: Auditor

Corridor Man: Howling
Corridor Man: Spa Day

The following are Corridor Man Boxsets:
Corridor Man Boxset 1-3
Corridor Man Boxset 1-5
Corridor Man Boxset 6-9

THANK YOU!

Contact the author:
- Email: mikefaricyauthor@gmail.com
- Twitter: @Mikefaricybooks
- Facebook: Mike Faricy Author
- Website: http://www.mikefaricybooks.com

Published by

MJF Publishing

www.ingramcontent.com/pod-product-compliance
Lightning Source LLC
Chambersburg PA
CBHW060402310726
48976CB00003B/913